I0603878

The Vintage Vendetta

A Franc Merlot Mystery

by

Brian L. Viers

Additional Books by the Author:

Silent Partner:
A True Story of Life, Death,
Crime and Surrender

Insights from Our Silent Partner

Significant U:
7-Steps to Becoming Simply Significant

Holy Smokes:
Faith, Fellowship, and Fire

Table of Contents

Prologue

Saint-Julien, Years Before the Mystery

There was always something slightly undone about Franc Merlot, as if he'd been poured into the wrong decade or left behind in a slower time. He wore his clothes with the kind of quiet precision that suggested not vanity, but respect— for fabric, for tailoring, for tradition. A navy sport coat clung to his lean but muscular frame, slightly creased at the elbows, and his signature ivory linen shirt always caught the breeze like a sail. His dark hair was thick but peppered with silver at the temples, and he rarely wore a hat unless the sun forced it. His hands—firm, precise—belied a lifetime of detailed work, of gently brushing truth from tangled lies. His years of work in France with DGSI, (General Directorate for Internal Security) had ended nearly a decade ago as he had moved into the private sector with less bureaucratic oversight.

What most noticed first, though, was his eyes. A deep, storm-touched gray with flecks of green, always half-narrowed in thought. Franc rarely smiled without reason. When he did, it wasn't performative, it was felt.

Carly Provost had once referred to him as a man built for dusk. It was the perfect time of day for Franc: moody, measured, in-between. The hours when cafés dimmed their lights, and the first bottle of wine was opened. That was when Franc was most alive.

Carly, by contrast, moved through the world with the confidence of someone who had already measured it and decided not everything needed solving. Tall, with honey-toned skin and waves of auburn hair she refused to tame, Carly wore casual elegance like a second skin. Always one step ahead of the next trend, yet never overly concerned with impressing anyone. Her laugh was rich, and when she laughed—truly laughed— it stopped conversations around her. There was something French about her spirit, though she'd been raised in the rolling countryside just outside Lyon.

They first met ten years before the vineyard mystery, in the quiet corner of a gallery opening in Marseille. Franc had been tailing a smuggler who had supposedly traded stolen Greek artifacts for forged Impressionist paintings. Carly had been attending to support a friend, the artist. The gallery's champagne was underwhelming, and the crowd was a bit too pleased with themselves.

They both reached for the same miniature Camembert tart.

Their hands brushed.

"Pardon," Franc said.

"You have good taste," Carly replied, taking the last tart and offering him half with a grin.

He let out a rare, subtle laugh. "Clearly, so do you."

Here they also discovered each had a strong passion for coffee and could drink it throughout the day or night.

What followed was a shared hour of murmured commentary, pointed observations, and the subtle, mutual awareness of two people who saw more than they said. Carly, as it turned out, was already familiar with Franc by reputation—he was the former detective from the coast who now preferred small cases in wine country. And Franc, who never forgot a face, remembered her from an article years earlier about a woman consulting on vineyard branding strategies across southern France.

The Camembert tart became a private joke—and later, a quiet kind of pact. They had remained loosely connected ever since, reuniting on occasion for wine festivals, gallery events, and—more recently—occasional investigations. She never demanded details but always understood the stakes.

She was the only one Franc trusted to be both a sounding board and a compass when the truth blurred. And though they were never officially anything more than friends, there were moments—quiet ones—when Franc imagined what life might have looked like if things had gone differently. If the sea hadn't stolen someone he loved. If he'd let it all in again.

But for now, they are partners, just passing through, and understanding the world.

And sometimes, solving its mysteries.

So, when a quiet American tourist vanishes amid the vineyard-covered hills of Saint-Julien, Detective Franc Merlot—semi-retired, but never quite out of the game—is drawn back into a world of whispered deals, forged art, and rivalries steeped in soil and secrets. Joined by his longtime confidante Carly Provost, Franc must navigate a labyrinth of false leads: a high-society watch dealer in Nice, an aging widowed socialite with a taste for gossip, and a centuries-old land dispute with modern consequences.

As the duo follows the trail from Bordeaux's sun-kissed vines to the glittering coast of Monaco, they begin to realize the disappearance may have less to do with art and everything to do with land—and the old money that still owns much of it.

From yacht parties to backroom deals, The Vintage Vendetta delivers a sun-drenched mystery layered with charm, tension, and sharp wit. With the elegance of a fine wine and the slow-burn intrigue of a noir classic, Franc Merlot's first adventure is both a love letter to French culture and a warning: in places where history and tradition runs deep, the truth is often buried just below the surface.

The Vintage Vendetta is the first in a new Franc Merlot series, perfect for readers who enjoy luxurious travel locations, and mysteries best

served with a touch of class, a swirl of
complexity, and a glass of something red.

Chapter 1

A Bottle in Bordeaux

The sunrise over Château des Vents unfolded without hurry, spilling amber and rose hues across the rolling vineyards of Saint-Julien. A light breeze carried the scent of ripening grapes and damp earth, a reminder of the steady rhythm of the seasons in this storied corner of Bordeaux. Franc Merlot stood at the edge of the stone terrace, hands tucked into the pockets of his linen jacket, watching as the morning mist retreated from the valley.

Always an early riser, Franc had long since abandoned the luxury of unnecessary sleep. Retirement, if you can refer to it, had not dulled his sense of routine, nor had it quieted the part of him that sought purpose in the day's unfolding events. Some men, upon stepping away from their first careers, sought leisure in idle pursuits. Franc, however, found himself restless. It had been several months since he returned to the Médoc, lingering longer than usual in a region that had once been a brief respite from his mundane governmental intelligence work.

Saint-Julien had a way of keeping people—Like both people and vines rooted themselves deep into the rich French soil. The vineyards stretched like patchwork across the hills, each estate with its own history, its own claim to legacy. It was a place where time moved deliberately, dictated by the vines and the hands that tended them. Franc visited often throughout the years and had always admired the precision of it—the patience required to perfect a craft that would not reveal its savory rewards for many years. And in many ways, it mirrored his own former profession.

Though no longer bound by the demands of a case, Franc remained a man of observation. It was a habit, really—the quiet assessments, the way he took in details others missed. He had spent his life unraveling complexities, fitting together fragments of truth until a story revealed itself. Now, in the absence of investigations, he found himself studying other things: the perfect pour of an espresso, the balance of flavors in a well-aged Pauillac, the mechanical perfection of a vintage automobile, the unspoken rivalries between winemakers that often ran deeper than their roots.

His interests had always been varied—an appreciation for fine food and wine, an eye for classic craftsmanship, a love for travel that had taken him from the limestone cellars of Burgundy to the bustling markets of Marrakesh in Morocco. But among all his passions, there was one that had eluded him for years: understanding how to quiet the past.

A faint tightening of his jaw betrayed the thought. He reached for the vintage, 1986 stainless Rolex Explorer on his left wrist, admiring the creamy white colored numerals on the dial before adjusting it absently, then quickly shaking off the creeping memories. The past had a way of finding its own time to resurface, but this morning, Franc had no intention of indulging it.

Instead, he turned toward the worn dusty path that led into town. A familiar café awaited him there, where the espresso was strong, the croissants buttery and flaked at the touch, and the day's first conversations unfolded over the sound of patron's chatter and the burr grinding of the machine for each next coffee order. It was a ritual he had come to reason with, if not, enjoy. A momentary escape from the questions that never fully left him.

With one last glance at the horizon, Franc Merlot stepped into the morning.

The café offered Franc a couple of hours of caffeinated indulgence as he contemplated his options for the day. He had arrived early, when only a handful of locals were about—bakers setting out fresh loaves, shopkeepers sweeping their thresholds, and the occasional vineyard worker stopping in for a quick espresso before heading to the vines. Now, as the morning stretched on, the quiet hum of the café had given way to a livelier rhythm. The sun, having finally climbed above the tiled rooftops, cast long, dappled shadows across the narrow streets.

Franc sat at his usual spot by the window, his coffee cup resting on the saucer, untouched for the past few minutes. He had been watching the town wake up, taking in the unhurried ease with which the day unfolded. Saint-Julien had a deliberate pace, one dictated more by the seasons than by the clock. Even as visitors trickled in, drawn by the promise of world-class wines and idyllic landscapes, the locals carried on as they always had—never rushed, never hurried.

He exhaled, settling deeper into his chair. The weight of years spent chasing leads, untangling motives, and piecing together the truth had left him with a tendency to expect urgency where there was none. Here, urgency didn't exist. A conversation could take an hour, a meal an entire afternoon, and no one would think it was a waste of time. It was an adjustment; one he was still wrestling over to make.

Franc glanced at the Bordeaux Gazette spread open before him. The pages rustled slightly in the breeze drifting in from the square. A mention of a local food and wine festival caught his eye—an annual celebration of the region's culinary and viticultural heritage, promising grand tastings, seasonal pairings, and a tour of some of the smaller vineyards rarely open to the public.

He considered the idea. Playing the tourist wasn't something he usually entertained, but perhaps today, it wouldn't be the worst idea. He could call one of the local guides, join a small group, and allow himself to indulge in the experience— observe without purpose, wander without intent.

Just as he reached for his phone, a familiar voice pulled him from his thoughts.

"You look like a man deep in contemplation," said a voice from behind him.

Franc turned, already recognizing the light, an amused tone before he even laid eyes on her. A popular local and one of his oldest friends in France, Carly Provost stood just inside the café's antique metal doors, hands on her hips, studying him with the knowing smirk of someone who had known him long enough to recognize when he was overthinking something.

"I was just deciding how to spend my day," he said, setting his phone down.

"And naturally, you needed coffee and hours of brooding to reach a conclusion?" she teased, sliding into the chair opposite him without waiting for an invitation.

Franc smirked but didn't deny it. How have you been? You look great as always." He continued. "I was considering the wine festival."

"Thank you, I've been busy, in much need for a holiday, but still finding ample time to enjoy the vines." She smiled. "And… good choice for the festival. The wine's good, the company's better, and if you're lucky, you might even learn something. I think I'll go, if you're asking. I'm always up for a bottle of wine in Bordeaux." She stated enthusiastically, more matter of fact than question.

"Of course. But I think I know enough about wine." Franc commanded.

Carly raised an eyebrow. "Oh? So, you know which château has been feuding with their neighbor for three generations? Or which winemaker has been secretly sourcing grapes from across the river to tweak his blends?"

Franc throwing up his hands, "I stand corrected."

"Let's do it!," she said, signaling the waiter for a cappuccino with raw sugar on the side. "If nothing else, it'll give you a chance to settle into the rhythm of things here. You're still adjusting, aren't you?"

Franc didn't answer immediately. He had spent his life moving from one case to the next, never allowing himself the luxury of idleness. Even now, with no pressing obligations, he still found himself searching for something—a thread to pull, a question to answer.

But perhaps today, he could let that go.

"I suppose a festival is as good a way as any to get acclimated," he said at last.

Carly smiled, raising her cup in an unspoken toast. "Now you're starting to understand Bordeaux."

Carly and Franc continued in casual conversation, just catching up on life as she savored her cappuccino, the frothy foam clinging to the edges of her cup. She had a way of keeping things light, effortlessly drawing Franc into conversation that felt both familiar and refreshingly effortless. It was one of the reasons he enjoyed her company—there was no pressure to be anything other than what he was in the moment. Carly might have been the closest thing Franc had in female companionship since losing an intimate partner nearly a decade ago in a random boating accident. Hence, his apprehension to go out on the water.

Franc, however, had reached his morning limit for caffeine. He glanced at his empty cup, considering how quickly the afternoon's tour would provide a change in beverages, something fuller, richer, more in line with the indulgences Bordeaux was known for. Red was his color. Any Medoc or Left Bank region Cabernet Sauvignon would do.

"You know," Carly mused, setting her cup down, "you should try to enjoy today without analyzing everything."

Franc smirked. "I analyze everything by habit. Occupational hazard."

"Right," she said, tilting her head. "Because strolling through vineyards, tasting world-class wines, and indulging in regional delicacies is exactly the same as solving a case."

"Maybe not exactly," Franc admitted, "but there's always something to notice. People, their habits, their interactions—especially in a setting like this."

Carly sighed playfully. "Fine. Observe all you want. Just promise me you won't treat this like some kind of undercover investigation."

"I promise nothing," Franc said with a smirk, earning an exasperated shake of the head from Carly.

With their plan set, they settled the bill and stepped outside, where the midday sun had begun to warm the stone streets. The festival awaited them, a celebration of the region's rich history and indulgences, promising good wine, good food, and, if Franc's instincts were correct, more than a few interesting stories hidden between the vines.

Chapter 2

Le Grande Wine Tour

As they walked toward the meeting point, Carly glanced at him with a knowing look. "This will prove to be a great day. By the way, I heard Mario Blanc might be at the festival today."

Franc exhaled slowly, adjusting the cuffs of his jacket. "Of course he is."

"Still think you won't find anything to investigate?", she teased.

Franc only chuckled. The day might have started as a simple exercise in relaxation, but now, he wasn't so sure.

The tour began at a leisurely pace, weaving through the sun-drenched vineyards where rows of vines stood in perfect formation, their leaves rustling lightly in the afternoon breeze. Franc found himself fully enjoying the experience— the warmth of the sun, the earthy aroma of the soil, and, most notably, the company of Carly. She had a way of making even the simplest moments feel effortlessly engaging, and he appreciated her enthusiasm for the region's history and indulgences.

They moved from one stop to the next. An open-roof small van, (almost resembling a bus), offered six bench-style seats for transporting up to 18 guests, sampling great wines that carried the weight of generations, each vintage telling a story of the land from which it came. The guide spoke animatedly about the unique terroir of Saint-Julien, explaining how even the slightest variations in soil composition and elevation could produce subtle differences in taste. Franc listened, somewhat relating the findings to his vast knowledge of coffee farms to draw comparisons, absorbing the details, though his attention occasionally drifted—old habits were hard to break.

It wasn't until they reached the third tasting that he caught something that pulled his mind away from the pleasures of the afternoon.

A small group of tourists had gathered near one of the oak barrels, their voices low but pronounced. Franc wasn't one to eavesdrop—at least, not without good reason—but the mention of the word "disappearance" piqued his curiosity.

"…just vanished," one of them said. "A hotel concierge staff member said he's been here for weeks, but no one's seen him since yesterday morning."

"You'd think someone would have noticed something," another chimed in. "I mean, it's not exactly a big town."

"Maybe he just left," a third voice offered. "People move on all the time."

"Without checking out? Without telling anyone? And without his belongings?" The first man shook his head. "Something's happened to him."

Franc sniffed, then swirled the deep red liquid, watching the way the light caught its edges as he observed the wine legs down the inside of his glass. A missing tourist—an American, no less. He had spent enough time in the region to know that disappearances were rare. Visitors came for the wine, the scenery, the escape, but they almost always left on their own terms.

His mind flickered back to Carly's words earlier in the café.

"Mario Blanc is said to be in town and might be at the festival today." Carly mentioned.

Mario was another home grown on the left bank in Bordeaux with ties to everyone and everything—mostly that which blurred the lines of ethics or morals.

Franc and Mario have a history. Each having seemed interested in similar cases over the years, yet their intentions rival beyond even their own relationship. Franc knew better than to align himself or trust Mario.

Franc exhaled, his fingers tightening slightly around the stem of his glass. He hadn't seen Mario yet, but that didn't mean he wasn't lurking nearby, blending into the crowd just enough to remain unnoticed.

Carly nudged him lightly. "You're doing that thing again."

"What thing?"

"The thing where your eyes shift slightly, and I can tell your brain is no longer on wine and good company."

Franc smirked, setting his glass down. "Old habits."

She followed his gaze toward the tourists. "What is it?"

"An American tourist disappeared. Word's getting around."

Carly frowned. "Disappeared, as in…?"

"As in, hasn't been seen since yesterday." He glanced around, scanning the crowd. "And you mentioned Mario Blanc earlier."

Carly folded her arms. "You think there's a connection?"

Franc wasn't sure yet. But something about the timing unsettled him.

"Let's just say," he said, tilting his head toward the next stop on the tour, "I think this festival just got a little more interesting."

Chapter 3

A Day of Discovery

Franc woke early, as usual, but today he felt the need to break the morning routine. Instead of starting his usual espresso journey before sunrise, he opted for a walk. The streets of Saint-Julien were still relatively quiet, but for the always present vineyard workers heading toward the fields. The crisp morning air carried the scent of lavender and the distant salt of the Atlantic, a reminder that Bordeaux's pleasures stretched far beyond its vineyards.

This little holiday, as Franc considered it, had offered moments of respite—a chance to slow down, to indulge in fine delicacies and good conversations. Yet, no matter how much he tried to ease into the rhythm of the region, his mind remained restless. He was a detective at heart, and something about the missing American refused to let him go.

The latest word circulating through town only deepened his intrigue. The man—an American businessman—had supposedly been in Saint-Julien merely as a stopover, waiting for a new yacht delivery in Nice. He wasn't a local, nor a devoted wine enthusiast. He had been biding his time, tending to business matters before moving on.

But now, he was gone.

Franc turned down a narrow lane that led toward the river, hands tucked into the pockets of his jacket. A new yacht. Nice. The details weren't particularly unusual—many wealthy men spent their summers floating between harbors, slipping in and out of coastal cities without much notice.

But disappearances? That was another matter entirely.

His thoughts circled back to Mario Blanc. Franc hadn't spotted him at the festival, but that didn't mean Mario wasn't around. If there was gossip to be heard or loose ends to be found, Mario would be near them, waiting for his moment to slip in with a knowing smirk and a half-truth.

Pausing at the river's edge, Franc let his gaze settle on the water, dark and still in the early light. He had told himself he was done with investigations, that this trip was meant for leisure. But old habits were difficult to break.

Perhaps it was time to start asking questions.

Franc lingered by the river, watching as the early light shimmered across its surface. The missing American had been waiting for a yacht in Nice. And Mario Blanc—if he had indeed come to Saint-Julien for the festival—had also arrived from Nice.

Another link.

Coincidence was never something Franc put much faith in.

He turned away from the water and began walking back toward the heart of town, his pace measured but purposeful. If Mario was in town, he wouldn't be difficult to find. A man like Mario Blanc had a way of making himself known when it suited him.

But first, Franc needed more information. The details surrounding the missing man were still vague—rumors exchanged between travelers, nothing substantial. If he wanted answers, he needed to start with the places where people talked the most: the cafés, the market, and the small hotels where visitors passed through.

And if Mario Blanc had anything to do with it, Franc had no doubt their paths would cross soon enough.

Franc pulled out his phone and dialed Carly's number as he made his way back through the quiet streets. She answered on the second ring, her voice carrying a warmth that reminded him of the easy company they'd shared the day before.

"Well, if it isn't the great Franc Merlot," she teased. "Calling before he's even had his morning espresso? This must be serious."

Franc smirked. "Just wanted to thank you for yesterday. The tour, the company—it was exactly what I needed."

"That almost sounds like a proper compliment," Carly said. "Are you feeling all right?"

He chuckled. "Don't get used to it."

She laughed, and for a moment, Franc almost reconsidered what he was about to say. But instead, he pressed on.

"I was thinking we should have dinner tonight. Somewhere nice."

"A second outing? You really must be enjoying your time in Bordeaux," she said, but there was a pleased note in her voice. "I'd love to. Any occasion?"

Franc hesitated, glancing down the street where the morning bustle was beginning to stir. He could have told her the truth—that he might be leaving, that something about this missing American had taken root in his mind, pulling him south to Nice for answers. But he didn't.

"Just thought we should end the trip on a good note," he said smoothly.

Carly was quiet for a beat before replying, "That almost sounds like a goodbye."

Franc exhaled. She knew him too well. "Just dinner," he said lightly. "No overanalyzing, please."

"For now," she said, amusement laced in her words. "I'll choose the place, then. You just show up."

"Agreed," Franc said.

As they ended the call, he slipped his phone back into his pocket, his gaze shifting toward the road south. Nice was calling, and with it, the promise of answers. But for now, there was still one last night in Bordeaux—and perhaps, one last moment of quiet before the chase began.

The day unfolded at an unhurried pace, the way summer days in Bordeaux often did. The sun had risen high, casting warm golden light over the town's cobbled streets and sandstone buildings. Franc had every intention of taking it easy, of treating the day as a final indulgence before his mind became consumed with the pull of Nice.

Carly, true to form, had her own agenda. She spent the late morning wandering the markets, weaving between vendors selling everything from handcrafted jewelry to aged cheeses and bottles of small-batch wines. She enjoyed the art of selection—choosing just the right silk scarf, the perfect tin of French sea salt, or a bottle of rosé that she claimed would taste like summer itself. She let herself revel in the simple pleasure of the day, taking in the chatter of the vendors, the scent of fresh bread drifting from a nearby bakery, the way the light hit the rooftops just so.

Franc, meanwhile, had retreated to his favorite quiet corner of town—a café tucked away from the main square, where he could sit with a coffee and pretend, if only for a little while, that his mind wasn't already elsewhere.

He took a seat under the shade of a striped awning, letting his thoughts settle as he sipped his espresso. The past few weeks had been restful in their own way, but now, with the prospect of Nice on the horizon, he found himself tying up loose ends. A few phone calls, an email or two, the small administrative tasks that came with preparing for another journey. If this was truly a farewell to Bordeaux—for now, at least—he wanted to leave nothing unfinished.

But even as he focused on these last personal responsibilities, his mind drifted. The missing American. The yacht waiting in Nice. Mario Blanc. The threads of the mystery were loose but present, weaving together in ways that nagged at him. He didn't have all the pieces yet, but he had enough to know he wouldn't be able to let it go.

By late afternoon, the heat had mellowed, and Franc took a slow walk back toward his hotel, stopping only briefly to pick up a single bottle of wine—one he knew Carly would appreciate. If tonight was a goodbye dinner, he figured it should be a good one.

As the sun dipped lower, the town's rhythm shifted. The last of the market vendors packed up their stalls, and the cafés began to fill with patrons seeking an early aperitif. Franc checked his watch. Carly would be finishing her shopping soon; no doubt having selected the perfect dress for the evening.

For now, Franc allowed himself a rare luxury—he put the questions aside. Tonight would be about good food, good company, and whatever came next could wait until morning.

Chapter 4

Farewell Dinner

Back in his hotel room, Franc leaned back in the armchair, his eyes flickering between the television and the slow-moving hands of the clock. On the screen, France was locked in a tense football match against Italy, their age-old rivalry playing out in front of an electrified crowd. The stakes were high, the tension palpable, but Franc found himself only half-invested. His thoughts were split—between the game, the upcoming dinner, and the road that might soon take him to Nice.

He rolled the stem of an empty wine glass between his fingers, one he decided best not to fill, before staring absently at the television. He had asked Carly to dinner under the guise of a simple farewell, but as the evening approached, he found himself questioning his own motives. He had always valued their friendship—easy, unspoken, built on a shared appreciation for travel, fine things and clever conversation. But was there something more to it?

His mind attempted to wander past the boundaries of platonic dinner, but he caught himself. Carly was a great woman—smart, charming, confident. A man would be lucky to have her, and yet… Franc exhaled sharply, rubbing a hand across his jaw.

It wasn't Carly that held him back. It was himself.

The loss of his last love still lingered like a shadow at the edges of his life. He had kept relationships at a distance ever since, not out of disinterest, but out of something harder to define—an inability, perhaps, to open himself up to the possibility of that kind of loss again.

The crowd on the television erupted in cheers, jolting him from his thoughts. France had scored. The energy on the screen was infectious, but Franc barely registered it. He glanced at the clock again, readied himself to head out.

Tonight, he reminded himself, it was about good company, a fine meal, and a proper goodbye. Nothing more.

And yet, as he stood, glancing in the mirror to adjust his tie one final time, he couldn't quite shake the feeling that the evening ahead might prove more complicated than he intended.

The evening air carried the scent of warm bread and a whisper of the nearby vineyards as Franc walked toward the restaurant, his mind surprisingly at ease. He had spent enough time in Bordeaux to know its rhythm, to anticipate the gentle shift from afternoon leisure to the quiet hum of the dinner hour. He adjusted the cuff of his jacket, feeling the comforting weight of the bottle of wine in his other hand.

A block away from the restaurant, just as he turned the corner, he spotted Carly coming from the opposite direction. She had the same easy stride, the same air of quiet confidence that had always made her presence a natural fit in his life.

She saw him at the same moment, and a knowing smile spread across her lips. Franc smirked in return.

"Of course," she said, shaking her head slightly as she fell into step beside him. "Fifteen minutes early, as always."

Franc shrugged. "Punctuality is a virtue. And here I thought I might have the advantage tonight—arriving first, choosing the table with just the right ambiance."

Carly chuckled. "And deny me the same opportunity? We should've known we'd end up here at the same time."

They continued together, the gentle clatter of evening dinners filling the air as they neared the restaurant. Neither had won their unspoken race, neither able to claim victory in selecting the perfect spot.

As they reached the entrance, Franc held the door open for her. "Shall we, then?"

Carly glanced at him, her expression amused yet warm, "Let's see who finds the better seat first."

The evening, it seemed, was already off to a familiar and comfortable start. But whether it would remain so—or take on unexpected turns—was yet to be seen.

As soon as they were seated, before the waiter could even bring the wine list, Franc broke the quiet between them.

"I might be heading to Nice tomorrow," he said plainly, watching Carly's expression.

She arched a brow, her fingers lightly tracing the rim of her water glass. "That was fast. You were just starting to relax here."

Franc exhaled, leaning back in his chair. "Maybe too much. But something about that missing

American—it doesn't sit right with me. And Mario Blanc being in town at the same time? Feels like more than coincidence."

Carly studied him for a moment, then nodded slowly. "You're not just thinking about going, are you? You've already made up your mind."

He smirked, appreciating how well she knew him. "Something like that."

She sighed but didn't seem surprised. "And here I was hoping we'd have another day or two of long lunches and wine tastings before you went chasing shadows."

"There will be more of those," Franc assured her, though even he wasn't sure when.

Carly tilted her head, considering him. "Is it just curiosity? Or something more?"

Franc hesitated, swirling the water in his glass before answering. "I don't know yet. But I intend to find out."

The waiter arrived then, interrupting the moment with a charming greeting and an offer to start with an aperitif. Carly smiled at Franc before turning to the waiter.

"An uncork please, as I've brought a bottle of something special," he said. "Since it might be our last meal together for a while," Franc tilted his head and continued. "Something to remember Bordeaux by."

As the waiter stepped away, Carly leaned forward, her voice softer now. "Then let's make this a proper sendoff. No overthinking, no unfinished business."

Franc met her gaze, then lifted his glass in a silent toast. "To that, I can agree."

The clink of their glasses was soft but certain, echoing faintly above the ambient hum of the restaurant—quiet conversations, the occasional burst of laughter, and the rhythmic sound of silverware meeting porcelain. The light was low, golden, casting warm shadows across the table between them.

Carly reached for the menu, her expression shifting from sentiment to strategy. "So, what's our plan here, Merlot? One last indulgent meal? Or do we eat light in case your instincts are wrong and we're wine tasting again tomorrow?"

Franc grinned. "Let's not insult the local cuisine. Full indulgence. If I end up chasing ghosts in Nice, I'd like to go on a full stomach."

She nodded in approval, scanning the offerings with practiced ease. "In that case, you're starting with the duck confit tartlet, and we're sharing the foie gras."

Franc raised a brow. "Just like that? No negotiation?"

Carly smirked. "You're leaving, remember? Tonight, I'm in charge."

The wine arrived then—an elegant Saint-Émilion with just the right structure to handle both rich dishes and difficult conversations. The waiter poured with reverence, and Franc took the first sip. He closed his eyes briefly, savoring it.

"Perfect," he said. "If this was my last night in Bordeaux, I'd want it to taste exactly like this."

As the courses arrived, time began to blur. They spoke with ease—stories of old acquaintances, trips they never took, people they both quietly missed. The conversation drifted from nostalgia to teasing, then back again to the space that often remained unspoken between them.

At one point, as Carly described a chaotic vineyard dinner she'd once attended in Provence, she caught Franc watching her. His eyes were thoughtful, maybe even a little wistful.

"What?" she asked, pausing mid-sentence.

He shook his head with a small smile. "Just thinking how easy this all is with you. Even when you're bossing me around about foie gras."

Carly tilted her head. "That's because you let me. Most men don't."

Franc smirked. "Most men aren't me."

She lifted her glass again, eyes meeting his. "No. They're not."

The night stretched comfortably between them, neither in a rush to bring it to a close. And yet, as dessert arrived—dark chocolate mousse with flecks of sea salt and a hint of espresso—they both knew the evening was drawing to a quiet, inevitable end.

Franc leaned back, savoring the final bite, and let out a contented sigh. "You were right. The perfect sendoff."

Carly nodded, but her voice was soft. "So what happens next?"

He looked at her, the flicker of the candlelight catching in his eyes. "I follow the trail to Nice. See where it leads. But I'll be back."

"Promise?" she asked, not as a plea, but as a challenge.

Franc considered it for a moment, then gave her the only answer that felt honest.

"If the trail lets me."

And with that, the bill was paid, the wine bottle empty, and the future—like the night itself—left open to possibility.

Chapter 5

Arrival on the Promenade

Morning came early for Franc. The soft gray light filtering through the window of his hotel room reminded him that while Bordeaux had offered comfort and familiarity, Nice demanded curiosity and vigilance. He packed carefully—no wasted space, no unnecessary weight. Years of travel had taught him that simplicity left room for discovery.

The train ride south offered a calming rhythm, the countryside gradually giving way to sun-soaked coastlines and a brighter palette of blues and golds. Franc watched the changing scenery with a distant look, sipping an espresso he'd grabbed from the platform kiosk. By the time the train eased into the station at Nice-Ville, the Mediterranean air had already begun to change him—reviving something inside that Bordeaux had lulled into rest.

Stepping off the train, Franc took a deep breath. The salt in the air. The citrus trees that lined the boulevards. The slight hum of a city that moved at its own luxurious pace.

Nice had always been a place of contrasts for him—equal parts leisure and mystery, indulgence and shadow. He'd solved cases here before, enjoyed fleeting romances, and wandered side streets just for the joy of discovering a new café or rare vintage tucked away from tourists.

As he walked through the station and into the street, suitcase in hand, he allowed himself—just briefly—to play the tourist. He paused near a vendor selling handmade soaps and lavender sachets, nodding politely at the shopkeeper. He admired the sweeping architecture, the ornate iron balconies, the red tile roofs glowing in the sun.

Franc pulled out his sunglasses and put them on. "Still got it," he muttered to himself, amused at how easily the city welcomed him back.

But as he turned toward his hotel, his thoughts sobered. He hadn't come for nostalgia.

There was a man missing. A yacht expected but not yet seen. And a familiar nuisance—Mario Blanc—lurking in the edges of it all.

Tourist mode would have to wait.

For now, he needed answers. And Nice, for all its sunlight and charm, was ready to offer them—if he knew where to look.

The Hôtel Negresco, with its grand pink dome and view of the sea, would serve as Franc's refuge for the time being. Its opulence had always struck him as both extravagant and comforting— like an old friend who aged well but never lost their flair for drama. As the bellman wheeled his bag through the ornate lobby, Franc took in the familiar scene: chandeliers dripping with light, velvet furniture too beautiful to sit on, and art lining the walls like a curated museum of European indulgence.

He checked in with ease, offering only a slight smile and minimal small talk. The staff didn't pry, another reason he liked it here.

Later that evening, the promenade called to him. The Promenade des Anglais shimmered under the setting sun, couples strolled hand in hand, cyclists rolled past with ease, and the sea breathed against the shore in a slow, hypnotic rhythm. Franc walked alone, hands in pockets, the salt air tousling his hair. It was the kind of evening where everything felt just a touch cinematic.

But his mind wasn't ready to fully relax. As lovely as the Negresco and the promenade were, it was the Old Town area that had always held the true pulse of Nice—the secrets, the whispers, the stories worn into the stone.

He would go there next.

The old quarter was a labyrinth of narrow streets and ochre-colored walls, laundry hanging between windows like the flags of everyday life. Market stalls still lingered from earlier, their scents of cured meats, olives, and sun-ripened fruit mixing in the air. Franc knew that in Old Town, truth and rumor lived side by side. Nothing was ever truly forgotten there, just layered beneath centuries of habit.

He paused at a small café tucked into a corner near the Cours Saleya. Familiar. No sign, no menu posted, just the way he liked it. He stepped inside and ordered a pastis, sipping it slowly as he watched the street come alive with twilight energy.

If the missing American had wandered this part of the city, someone would remember. And if Mario Blanc had passed through, his presence, subtle or not—would have left a trail.

Franc's instincts stirred. It wasn't just about asking questions. It was about knowing which silence mattered, and which noise to ignore. Tomorrow, he'd start listening.

Chapter 6

Blue Chair Traditions

The morning came gently, with a pale sky stretching over the sea and the kind of stillness that only existed before the city fully woke. Franc walked quietly along the Promenade des Anglais, lost in thought, the soles of his shoes brushing rhythmically against the stone. The air was cooler than the afternoon sun would later allow, just crisp enough to keep him sharp.

He found his seat in one of the iconic blue chairs lined up like sentinels facing the horizon. The Mediterranean shimmered in layered shades of silver and blue, soft waves folding into the shore with effortless grace. A street vendor was just beginning to set up, and the scent of early croissants drifted faintly in the breeze.

Franc sipped his usual order; small double espresso, from the takeaway bar near the Negresco to start with, nodding a polite "merci" to the barista who had begun to recognize him already. He leaned back in a chair, letting the warmth of the cup anchor him. There was clarity in this routine, a quiet moment to reset before the day turned more complicated.

As Franc stepped through the shaded doorway of Café Lavande, the scent of fresh croissants and rich espresso met him like an old friend. The morning sun spilled in across the tiled floor, catching on the polished brass of the counter. A gentle bell above the door chimed his arrival, and before he could approach the register, a familiar voice rang out.

"Bonjour, Monsieur Merlot!"

Franc looked up to see a bright-eyed young woman behind the counter, her auburn ponytail swinging as she turned from the espresso machine. She wore the café's signature navy apron and a wide, familiar grin.

"Sylvie," Franc said with a tip of his head. "You remember me."

"Of course I do. You always order the same—double espresso, no sugar, and the butter croissant if it's before ten," she said proudly. "You've been coming in since spring, and you always sit by the window unless it's raining."

He chuckled. "I must be terribly predictable. If she only knew this was always my second stop of the morning."

"Consistent," she said, pouring the espresso with practiced ease. "It's kind of nice, actually. Makes the place feel steadier somehow."

Franc took the saucer and cup she offered and gave her a small nod of gratitude. "Well, Sylvie, I'll try not to ruin my reputation this morning."

She leaned slightly over the counter, lowering her voice. "You know, my aunt thinks you're some retired film star hiding out in Saint-Julien. I told her you're far too modest for that."

Franc smiled, amused. "Let her keep guessing. Mystery's more fun that way."

She winked. "I'll bring your croissant."

He scanned the horizon as if it might offer answers. The yacht—the missing American—the chance reappearance of Mario Blanc. All of it floated in his mind like puzzle pieces yet to find their borders.

By the time the sun fully rose, casting golden light over the mosaic walkways and the joggers now peppering the path, Franc stood. The city behind him was coming to life—shutters opening, café tables being wiped down, scooters whirring through tight alleys.

He straightened his jacket, tucked the small notebook he always carried into his pocket, and turned inland toward Vieux Nice.

Today, he would begin work.

He wasn't yet sure who to talk to, or what thread might unravel first—but Franc Merlot didn't need certainty. Just a place to start.

And Old Town, with all its layered history and half-kept secrets, had never let him down before.

Old Town

The day had been long and deliberate. Franc had worked his way through the hilly streets with the patience of a man both following a scent and leaving his own. He asked subtle questions, leaned into half-answers, and revisited shops he hadn't stepped inside in years—antique booksellers, dusty map traders, and jewelers with too few customers and too much discretion.

But it was in a quiet watch boutique just off Rue Paradis that things began to tick.

The shop was elegant, unassuming—its display windows filled with rare timepieces that whispered rather than boasted. Inside, the air was clean and cool, scented faintly with leather and brass polish. Franc greeted the owner, an older man with thin white hair and eyes as sharp as the loupes he wore on his collar.

They talked about watches at first. Franc feigned interest in a vintage Breguet, admiring the craftsmanship and lineage. But when he mentioned the American—a collector of sorts, he'd heard, with interest in rare chronographs—the owner stiffened slightly.

"There are collectors," the man said carefully, "and there are investors who pretend to be collectors. The difference is interest versus intent."

Franc tucked that line away. "Would this particular gentleman—mid-forties, well-funded, often seen near the port—fit into either category?"

A beat. Then a subtle nod. "He was here. Looked at a very specific piece I never put in the window."

Franc's gaze narrowed. "And did he buy it?"

"No," the man replied, glancing toward the door, "but he said he would return. Only he didn't."

That was two days before he'd reportedly vanished.

By evening, Franc found himself back at the hotel, reservations waiting for him at a quiet restaurant not far from the port. The maître d' recognized him from past visits and offered him a table in the corner, just the way he liked it— away from the view, near the shadows.

A bottle of Château Palmer 2000 was already breathing. It wasn't on the menu. He hadn't asked for it. And yet, here it was.

He smiled quietly. Someone was watching. Perhaps someone was helping.

He swirled the first pour, letting the wine tell its story—soft earth, black cherry, and the quiet confidence of time well kept. As the first course arrived, he made notes in his journal. Watch collectors, art buyers, and a financial undercurrent that hinted at something more: a laundering syndicate using high-value goods as currency. The kind of quiet trade that could run through hotels, auction houses, and yes—yacht sales.

He was halfway through his second course when a voice stopped him cold.

"You always eat this well when you're chasing ghosts?"

Franc looked up, surprised but not entirely displeased.

Carly Provost stood before him, windblown and radiant in a way only someone who belonged in the South of France could manage. She slid into the seat across from him without waiting for an invitation.

"Nice suits you," she said, accepting a glass of his wine she had arranged to be on his table waiting.

He raised an eyebrow. "You followed me?"

"No," she said, taking a sip. "I obviously beat you here. And I brought news."

Franc leaned in, the quiet clink of her new bracelet punctuating the pause. It also signaled she had been shopping.

She pulled a folded sheet of paper from her bag and placed it between them. "A copy of the yacht delivery manifest. The American's name is listed twice. But there's something strange. The second entry shows the same name, same boat, but with a different brokerage firm and departure port."

Franc stared at it; his instincts sharp. "Two deals. Two identities. Or someone tried to reroute him."

Carly nodded. "And Mario Blanc's name appeared on the marina guest list the same day the second paperwork was filed."

Franc sat back, exhaled slowly. So much for a quiet dinner.

Nice wasn't just a detour anymore—it was the center of the storm. And he wasn't walking out of it until he understood what, exactly, the American had gotten himself into… and who else wanted it buried.

Chapter 7

Parting Glasses

and Private Plans

Carly lingered over the last sips of wine as the restaurant emptied around them, the low hum of conversation giving way to the sound of waiters gathering glasses from neighboring tables. Franc appreciated her presence more than he could admit aloud—steady, unbothered by his obsessions, and always arriving just when the next door seemed too closed to push open alone.

But still, he had to say no.

"I appreciate the company," Franc said gently, folding the yacht manifest and slipping it into his jacket pocket. "And the information. But tomorrow, I must move a little… differently."

Carly didn't flinch. She smiled, knowing him well enough not to be offended. "I didn't come to shadow you, Franc. Just thought you'd want to see that paper in person—and I wanted a little view of the sea."

He leaned back, his expression softening. "You took the train down here just to bring me a document?"

She smirked. "I took the train for the wine, the water, and the weather. You were just a bonus." A pause. "But yes. I knew you'd want to see it for yourself. And I knew you wouldn't ask me to come."

He nodded slowly, the corner of his mouth lifting. "Thank you."

They left the restaurant together, just people watching as the local youth had engulfed the streets as the weather invited outdoor dining and activities. They peeked into windows making small talk, enjoying the energy around them before strolling another block.

"You'll call if you need anything?" she asked at the corner.

Before then parting ways—her to a modest boutique hotel near the train station, him toward the dim path that led back to the Promenade.

The night air carried the scent of salt and citrus, and the lamps overhead bathed the pavement in golden hues. It was an exciting time to be in the south of France. Franc often recalled his prior life and what it might have developed into if he had lived here more than what he had. An occasional month or two per holiday season.

Carly didn't push further. She placed a soft kiss on his cheek and turned with a playful, "Don't get lost in your own mystery."

And with that, she disappeared into the night, her steps as confident as her arrival.

Franc turned, hands in his pockets, the city behind him and the sea at his back. "Always", he spoke aloud beyond her earshot.

The next morning, he for once turned on the television for some local and world news updates. He had been removed from life as he knew it anyway, for weeks now while strangely following an occasional hunch of this case.

Franc, then satisfied by what coverage he caught on television for the couple of minutes he allowed his attention to, stood on the balcony of his hotel suite, coffee in hand and watched the early ferries pulling into port. The city below was already alive with motion—fruit vendors arranging crates, mopeds zipping through traffic, seagulls circling above the fish markets.

Carly's train would be rolling north by now. Or so Franc assumed. Her role in this chapter is complete—for now.

He didn't worry about Carly—She could take care of herself, that he knew. But chapters of his past and the tragic loss of a close female companion had since left him feeling somewhat responsible, or at least overprotective in current circumstances. Maybe one day life would deal him another hand to play but the prospects were nil.

He, however, had more ground to cover. He had an appointment with someone known only by a nickname: Le Furet—the ferret. A man who trafficked in secrets and operated just on the edge of respectable society. He had a penchant for knowing who came into Nice, who left, and who intended to stay beneath notice.

Franc finished his coffee and slipped the manifest back into his jacket pocket.

Today, the real hunt began.

Across town Carly leaned over the rail of the small private boat she'd chartered for the afternoon, her hair loosely pulled back, sunglasses framing her eyes as the warm sea breeze swept past her. The boat gently sliced through the waters off the coast of Nice, gliding just far enough from the port to offer a full view of the city's sun-kissed architecture rising behind the palm-lined Promenade des Anglais.

She took a deep breath, allowing the sun's rays to warm and darker her skin. The salt air carried hints of summer and memory. Nice was a place that unfolded itself slowly, like a luxury scarf—layer by elegant layer. And she was starting to wonder if she was ready to call it something more than just a place she passed through.

Earlier this morning, Carly had wandered through the markets of Cours Saleya, buying a bracelet and scarf, her favorite pastime when visiting. She'd picked up a bundle of fresh lavender, a few delicate soaps from a vendor she now greeted by name, the vintage scarf from a tucked-away boutique that felt more like treasure hunting than shopping. She'd even tried on a few flats in a shop she swore she'd never need, but the kind, vibrant shopgirl reminded her, "In Nice, even walking should feel like leisure."

And it did. Everything here felt different. Time passed slower, even when it wasn't. People watched more, talked longer, sipped things that tasted better than they remembered. Future pleasantries and fond memories were accumulating here with each day passing.

Later that evening, she had plans to meet a few new acquaintances—artists and gallery owners she'd been introduced to during an afternoon art unveiling party days earlier. They were now hosting an aperitif on a tucked-away rooftop terrace, the kind of gathering Carly always found herself slipping into easily.

She sat, barefoot on the boat's teak deck, the breeze on the water passed over her pink sun-soaked skin offering a cool reprieve, a linen wrap draped over her knees, she wondered: Could I do this more often? Could I really split time here? Or permanent residence? The thought lingered longer than it ever had before.

She thought of Franc and wondered if his day was as enjoyable as hers. Almost feeling guilty for not being with him but knew when he was in his element and focused on something, its best to step aside. She also knew he would be in touch soon and it wasn't personal.

Maybe dual residency would be an option? She allowed the notion of life here again to regain her thought process.

Work in Bordeaux could wait, at least for a while. Franc's cases always evolved slowly before snapping shut. And here—here there were things worth exploring. Not just the shops, or the sea, but a quieter version of herself she didn't often get to know.

Maybe it was nothing. Or maybe it was the beginning of something.

The boat turned gently toward the shore, and Carly smiled. Just in time for a glass of wine with her friends waiting on the marina dock.

Carly tucked a linen bag under her arm as she stepped off the passerelle onto dry land. The salt air still clinging to her body. The afternoon sunbathed the street in a golden hue, and she paused to let a group of tourists pass, her flats clicking faintly against her heels as she adjusted her sunglasses.

That's when she heard the voice.

"Carly? Carly Provost?"

She turned instinctively, eyes scanning until they landed on a man in a navy button-down, sunglasses perched atop windswept hair. It took her a beat to place him.

"Cameron?" she said, almost surprised to hear herself say it out loud.

Cameron Deveraux, a local resident in Bordeaux, and one of the quiet but observant guests from the wine tour she'd taken with Franc. He'd asked a few sharp questions at the vineyard—about soil quality, ownership transitions, and regional mergers that hadn't struck her as casual curiosity at the time. Now, standing here in Nice of all places, he looked every bit the part of someone who blended into high-end settings with practiced ease.

"What are you doing here?" she asked with a smile that was friendly but cautious.

He shrugged; his grin easy. "Work… or something like it. And you?"

"Just enjoying Nice," she said, careful not to say too much. "Taking a little break."

"From Bordeaux or from the detective?" he asked, a flicker of amusement in his voice.

She raised an eyebrow but didn't answer. "It's a lovely city."

"That it is," he said, falling into step beside her as she turned to walk. "You know, I was surprised to see you on that wine tour. Not your usual crowd."

Carly looked over at him. "And yet, here you are in mine again."

He laughed, smoothly and low. "Touché."

They stood in an uncomfortable silence for a moment, the sounds of the city weaving around them, clinking glasses from a café nestled on the water's edge at the marina, the distant hum of a motorbike, gulls crying over the shoreline.

"You still into wine?" she asked casually.

Cameron's expression shifted just slightly. "Always. Some vintages never quite leave you."

Looking towards a group of friends nearby, she stopped mid sentence shifting thought. "Well, it was nice seeing you again, Cameron. Enjoy the rest of your… work."

He tipped his head. "Same to you, Carly."

As he turned and walked down the street, Carly watched him go, the sound of his steps fading. Something about the run-in stayed with her longer than it should have. Maybe it was nothing.

But in Nice, maybe nothing was ever really just that.

Chapter 8

The Widow on the Wind

The sun had barely reached its peak when Franc found himself back in the familiar tangle of Vieux Nice. He had time before his meeting with Le Furet and chose to walk the long way—through the flower market, past the cafés already buzzing with late breakfast crowds, and around the corner of Place Garibaldi where elegance often brushed elbows with scandal.

It was there, stepping out of a pale silver vintage Citroën, that she appeared.

Claudine Bellecôte.

Even in motion, she carried the stillness of wealth—measured, composed, aware of being observed but never needing to react to it. She wore oversized red sunglasses, and a silken scarf tied at her throat like a final flourish to a painting. Her widowhood, the city had long decided, had only added to her allure.

Everyone in Nice—and along most of the Riviera—knew of her. Some claimed she had inherited vineyards near Eze; others whispered she had been married to a shipping tycoon or a disgraced politician, depending on which cocktail party one attended. What they agreed on was that Claudine was always invited, always remembered, and never quite understood.

"Franc Merlot," she said with the sort of warmth that suggested she knew more than she should. "What a delicious surprise."

Franc turned, offering a small bow of acknowledgment. "Madame Bellecôte. Still defying the ordinary, I see."

Her lips curled into a smile. "Is that a compliment or an accusation?"

"That depends," he said, "on whether you're hiding or simply observing."

Claudine laughed lightly, the sound floating above the street noise. "I've never hidden a day in my life, my dear. I just find it… strategic to appear when the moment is most interesting."

She linked her arm through his without asking. "Walk with me. I've heard things. About yachts. About Americans. And about someone from Nice who's not being quite so subtle anymore."

Franc felt the shift instantly—Claudine was playing the game, but on her own board. He knew better than to trust her, yet he'd be foolish not to listen.

They strolled slowly, the crowd parting around them like waves around a pier. "You've heard about the American?" he asked, tone cautious.

"Darling," she purred, adjusting her sunglasses, "in this city, one doesn't need to hear much. One simply notices who stops attending the usual soirées. And more importantly, who starts asking the wrong questions afterward."

Franc raised an eyebrow. "And who might that be?"

Claudine smiled. "You. And a man from the port who goes by Le Furet. Be careful with him. He smells desperation better than a shark senses fear in the water."

They paused at a corner café, where she ordered a champagne flute and insisted Franc join her for just ten minutes. "For appearances, of course," she said. "A gentleman seen in public with a woman of my reputation is far less likely to be noticed asking questions."

Franc chuckled under his breath. "And what is your reputation exactly?"

Claudine leaned in, her expression unreadable. "I outlive everyone. That tends to keep people guessing."

They clinked glasses.

A few steps closer to the truth, Franc thought.

And another mystery to follow.

Chapter 9

Reflections and Invitations

That night, back in the cool quiet of his room at the Negresco, Franc sat in the deep armchair by the window, a glass of Armagnac in hand, the lights of the promenade flickering below like whispers across the sea. The day had been a study in coincidence—or something much more crafted.

Claudine Bellecôte.

She entered the scene with elegance, but Franc had seen enough veiled truths to know when a conversation was a performance. The timing of her arrival. The way she referenced Le Furet. The ease with which she dropped breadcrumbs without offering the whole loaf. It all felt rehearsed. Or worse—coordinated.

Franc fumbled for the remote control and turned on the television, then turned the channel to a classic French melody for background noise. He wanted to rest before considering his next move.

His plan to grab a few minutes of shut eye hadn't come together as hoped. Too much on his plate and multiple leads in different directions seemed more hindrance than anything. In his profession leads were just that—leads. Ironically, often misleading.

Back to square one as he began to look at how everything initially came about. He considered sequences, locations, tangibles, human involvement and how each part could align with another. A process he cherished over the years for fresh perspectives when stalled in a case.

He stared out toward the water, swirling the glass slowly.

The yacht manifest, the missing American, the whispers about art collectors and watch syndicates… And now Claudine, a woman so wrapped in society's fabric she practically wove it. Too much lined up too neatly. As if someone wanted him to follow this trail—but not too quickly.

On the side table sat the slim ivory invitation she had slipped him just before parting.

La Soirée des Couleurs — a charity gala for coastal preservation, held annually at the Villa Beaujour. The guest list, Franc knew, would be more glittering than the chandeliers. Wine magnates. Art brokers. International investors. And more than a few ghosts in polished shoes. That guest list would be objective number one to acquire that night.

He turned the card over again, reading the handwritten note scrawled at the bottom in elegant, feminine script:

"Curiosity deserves company. I'll save you a dance." — C.B.

Franc smirked and rocked back in the chair. "Who is this woman?" He asked himself.

This gala might not solve the puzzle. But it could light up the pieces that were still in shadow.

At least provide a semblance of proximity. Process of elimination would have to happen. He needed the guest list.

He took another sip, the slow burn grounding him.

Tomorrow, he'd prepare for the weekend.

But tonight—he let the city speak in silence. A nap wasn't in play for Franc but allowing his body to rest in place was the next best thing. And the ambiance and drink choice tonight had definitely set the mood right.

He'd certainly drift off soon.

Chapter 10

Preparation and Pleasure

Franc rose early, feeling good. The rest was welcomed, now the golden light of the Riviera filtering softly through the curtains of his room at the Negresco. The city was already stretching itself awake—the muted sound of shopkeepers lifting shutters, the rhythmic sweep of brooms along the promenade, and the distant scent of espresso brewing just beyond the square.

Today was for preparation. Tomorrow, a spectacle.

But first—breakfast.

He dressed casually for the morning—crisp white linen shirt, sleeves rolled, light stone trousers, and soft leather loafers with no socks. No need for formalities today. He headed down to a modest café tucked just a block behind the hotel, a place called Café Boulanger de la Mer—known more to locals than tourists.

He ordered a simple but satisfying plate: a soft-boiled egg with sea salt and chives, a wedge of herbed goat cheese, and a warm croissant, so flaky it practically whispered as he tore into it. The coffee was dark and sharp, with a splash of warm milk—the way it had been made for generations.

He lingered over breakfast, scanning the quiet street. Tourists would soon fill the sidewalks, but for now, it was Nice at its gentlest.

With no particular urgency, Franc set out on foot through the city. He passed the pastel buildings of the old town, their shutters cracked just wide enough to catch the breeze. Wrought iron balconies overflowed with flowers—red geraniums, climbing ivy, and little citrus trees in clay pots.

At the Cours Saleya market, he wandered under the striped awnings, sampling from stalls like a seasoned local. A wedge of socca—the savory chickpea flatbread still warm from the griddle— was his first indulgence. Then he picked up a handful of candied orange peels from a sweet vendor who swore by her grandmother's recipe. He tucked them into his pocket for later.

At a small men's boutique near Place Masséna, Franc browsed with purpose. The gala demanded presence. He settled on a sharply tailored midnight blue dinner jacket with a subtle black silk shawl collar. Underneath, he'd pair it with a fine white shirt, French cuffs, and a slim black tie—not quite a bowtie, not quite traditional. Something modern, something respectful. Shoes, polished leather, Italian-made, completed the look.

He added a pocket square in a muted wine color. A small nod to Saint-Julien.

As he walked back along Rue Paradis, he stopped into a perfumery, selecting a discreet bottle of vintage cologne—notes of bergamot, cedar, and a trace of tobacco. Familiar. Grounded. Something that lingered just long enough.

He paused for a moment at Place Rossetti, watching children dart in and out of the fountain while an elderly couple argued lovingly over gelato flavors. Franc smiled to himself. Even amidst a sea of elegance and intrigue, life had a way of reminding you of what really mattered.

The breeze along the Promenade des Anglais was just beginning to lift, teasing the sea into soft waves as Franc strolled at an unhurried pace. The early light had softened the city's edges, casting a silver hue across the Mediterranean and against the façades lining the promenade. He passed morning joggers, couples sipping coffee on shaded terraces, and artists already staking out corners with their easels.

Then he paused.

Tucked along the promenade, near the Quai des États-Unis, stood a small but instantly recognizable figure — the miniature replica of the Statue of Liberty. Only four feet tall, it still bore the same dignified presence, holding the familiar torch high into the blue sky.

Franc approached it slowly, his hands in his coat pockets. The original, gifted from France to the United States in 1886, had always stood as a symbol of alliance, welcome, and the pursuit of freedom. This little version, a quiet nod to shared ideals, now stirred something deeper within him.

He thought of the missing American—vanished from Saint-Julien under questionable circumstances. A man who, for all intents and purposes, had vanished like a whisper. And yet, something about this statue, this moment, made Franc wonder if the man had simply chosen to disappear. Or been given reason to.

The torch, though small, seemed to point not just toward the sea, but toward possibility. Maybe even a direction. Franc lingered a moment longer, reading the plaque beneath the statue, noting the quiet pride etched into its history.

A gift of liberty. A symbol of connection. A mystery now tying two countries again.

He narrowed his eyes toward the horizon. The more he thought about it, the more it felt like a clue.

By the time he returned to the hotel, his arms held bags of treats and essentials. He laid everything out across the bed—crisp cufflinks, his carefully folded suit, a handwritten note from Carly he'd kept tucked in his wallet. Just a line she'd written once: "Stay curious, and don't be reckless."

He sat in the armchair once more, this time with a chilled glass of rosé from Provence. The day was calm. The city is still generous.

Tomorrow, the masks will come out.

But tonight, again called for rest. And to remember who he was before the game began.

Chapter 11

The Eve of Revelations

Evening fell softly over Nice, casting a rose-hued glow across the terracotta rooftops. Franc stood at the window of his room, glass in hand, looking out over the Promenade des Anglais as the sea shimmered in deep indigo under the fading light.

He had always appreciated a city's rhythm. Each place had its own pulse at twilight. In Nice, the mood slowed and smoldered. The streets, once bustling with chatter and commerce, now gave way to a more deliberate crowd and energy. Couples drifted from boutiques to brasseries, friends gathered over aperitifs, and a hush settled over the balconies as candles were lit and dinners served.

Franc set his glass down and took his time dressing. The jacket fit precisely, hugging his shoulders with just enough weight to remind him of the man he was—and the man he had once been. He adjusted the pocket square, fixed the cuffs, and slipped the watch onto his wrist—a gift from an old friend, now long gone, its face a soft champagne gold.

Before heading out, he folded Carly's note again and tucked it into the inside pocket of his jacket. A quiet token. A reminder not to chase shadows without a tether.

Rather than a car, Franc chose to walk to the Villa Beaujour, located just past the port in the hills above the city. The route was winding and fragrant, lined with flowering vines and olive trees. The light breeze off the sea made the uphill stroll manageable, even pleasant, and the anticipation of the night ahead stirred something not unlike adrenaline in his chest.

Arriving at the villa gates, he found the event already in full swing. Laughter and live jazz floated into the air as torches flickered along the drive. A valet in a crisp white jacket nodded and ushered Franc through the grand arch and past what appeared to be the finest collection of limousines and supercars one event could possibly bring together. The current value of the parking lot lined with such treasures now rivaled many small city depositories.

The garden had been transformed into a dream. Whispered rumors of attendance expected by some Monaco royalty may have embellished this decor design. It was an event unparalleled even by the highest of standards set in the Riviera.

Soft lights strung above the terrace, elegant guests dressed in various degrees of old-money restraint and nouveau flair. The finest wine was being poured from crystal decanters into thin-stemmed glasses. The aroma of truffle oil, grilled sea bass, and fresh herbs danced from the catering tables. Elegance exudes itself from every angle.

The guest list was imperative.

Franc moved with measured steps, taking it all in. He wasn't just attending—he was studying. Watching who spoke to whom, who hovered at the edges, who made eye contact and who avoided it.

And then, near the central sculpture, he saw her—Claudine Bellecôte. Draped in a satin gown the color of midnight, adorned with pearls so casually elegant they seemed born with her. She turned and spotted Franc, raising her glass in a silent toast before gliding toward him with the confidence of someone used to commanding a room.

"You clean up well, Monsieur Merlot," she purred.

"And you're punctual for a dance," he replied, offering his arm.

As they drifted into the music and the mystery of the night, Franc knew one thing: this evening wasn't merely a gala. It was a stage. Most attendees here only came to such events with a purpose, at this level, no longer just needing to be seen.

Stories followed whether warranted or not. Lifestyles here came with that price tag. Some relishing the notoriety, others defiant to the unknown tabloid media telling their sides of a story before verifying facts. The US media was the leader in such malignant behavior.

And everyone here had something to hide. Even if they didn't know it.

Franc moved through the crowd with practiced grace, his every step deliberate yet unhurried. The Villa Beaujour—perched like a crown above the sea—was nothing short of cinematic theatre tonight. Columns draped in jasmine, servers in tuxedos offering trays of oysters, caviar and champagne, and laughter that seemed always on the edge of saying too much.

It was the kind of event where reputations were forged, or undone, over an offhand comment by the rosé table. Such decorum was learned early in life and expected by this class of player.

Franc nodded respectfully to the familiar faces—winemakers from Provence, a retired French actor known more now for his eccentric paintings than his films, American actors, turned political activists, a Monaco shipping magnate with a rumored interest in lost art, and an Italian countess who made it a habit to spend her summers in the hills above Cannes.

They were the who's who of the Côte d'Azur—wealthy, worldly, and wonderfully evasive.

He sipped slowly, accepting the occasional compliment on his suit, even engaging in light conversation about the vintage being served—an elegant Saint-Émilion he found impressively balanced for such a showy event. But beneath the smile, Franc was working. Listening. Watching.

At the center bar, he caught a brief exchange between two distinguished older men in sharp dark suits. One wore an overly conspicuous emerald ring on his thick left-hand pinky finger; the other, a vintage chronograph watch nearly identical to one he'd seen listed as missing in a registry of high-value thefts.

Their conversation was hushed and in English—American, New York accents—but their body language said more than words. They crossed paths more than once with the American actors, exchanged looks and then went their own ways. It looked suspiciously like communication to Franc but without verbally speaking. Franc wanted their names for certain.

He used his phone camera to secretly take pictures and videos but was careful not to be observed in the act.

He made mental notes—names half-heard, brands dropped too casually, one mention of "private inventory" that didn't sit right.

Claudine found him again, effortlessly slipping her hand into the crook of his arm. "Enjoying the night, or just cataloguing everyone's sins?"

Franc smiled. "Can't a man do both?" He added, "I think I could get along pretty well with most of these folks, wouldn't you agree?", he smiled.

She chuckled for good measure, then leaned in. "You see the man by the statue? Grecian jawline, dreadful powder blue tie?"

Franc followed her gaze and nodded.

"That's Henri Duval. Supposedly a philanthropist. But ask anyone who lost a rare painting after the Paris floods last year who really handled the insurance sales."

"A name worth remembering," Franc said, sipping, before sneaking a few pictures.

"And another," she added, lowering her voice. "The gentleman who arrived late—tall, grey temples, Swiss cufflinks? He's not on the official guest list."

Franc's eyes narrowed slightly. "What is he, then?" The mention of the guest list again reminded him of his mission.

"About that guest list Claudine, how would you know he isn't on it? I don't see an official list at the door." Franc baited her in hope of discovering the whereabouts of a physical list.

Claudine smiled faintly. "What we all are, dear Franc. Interested parties. That's what he is too."

Franc's shoulders slumped as his fact finder had failed—this time.

The band shifted to a slower tune. Conversations deepened. The air became heavier with meaning.

Franc excused himself and drifted along the perimeter, pausing occasionally at displays of auction items. Framed photographs from the 1920s. Signed wine bottles from now-defunct châteaux. A sculpture listed under "anonymous donor," which he knew immediately was a forged Giacometti.

This wasn't just a charity gala. This was an open market for closed-door deals.

It was behind the auction tables where he scored. The "list", an attendance roster meant merely for invoicing the buyers after the winning bids closed. Two crisp white papers full of names only. Franc wanted to grab the two sheets and exit the event inconspicuously but thought better of it and eventually found enough separation from the wealthy bidders to snap photos of each with being noticed.

Mission accomplished.

He then saw Mario Blanc briefly, across the room, laughing too hard with a group of lesser nobles and art agents. Franc didn't approach. Deciding best to keep his distance. For now. But the sight of Mario here confirmed something: the missing American had connections that reached further into the Riviera than he initially guessed.

Franc leaned against a stone balustrade as the ocean shimmered below. Looking at his watch wondering how much time before he'd be held captive pretending to be interested.

He stepped outside on the balcony, cut and lit a Davidoff Churchill, Late Hour cigar, an old habit he indulged on nights like this. This act would buy an hour, he thought.

Pleasure and purpose danced dangerously close. His cigar had drawn outsiders to strike up conversation with him and indulge in whatever their desired smoke of choice. Conversations flowed loosely. His choice for a cigar had proven lucrative.

And in the midst of gold dresses, whispered transactions, and too-sweet champagne, Franc Merlot reminded himself why he was here.

To find the truth, whatever face it wore.

Chapter 12

Sunlight and Shadows

The morning light spilled into Franc's suite at the Negresco, golden and warm, casting soft edges on the day's uncertainty. He had risen early, the echoes of the gala still humming in his mind— names, glances, overheard remarks. He combed through his photos on the phone, zooming in for anything but for now coming up empty.

The list would take further consideration. A great fact-finding project for Carly through local records would be required.

It was like piecing together a fine vintage: each note subtle, requiring patience and palate.

He stepped out onto the balcony with his espresso, sea breeze brushing past his collar. With the Mediterranean unfolding before him, it might have seemed like a morning for rest. But for Franc, rest was a luxury rarely indulged when intuition whispered otherwise.

He dialed Carly.

"Morning, Merlot," she answered, sounding both amused and alert.

"Didn't sleep in?"

"I did. But I also know your calls never come without reason."

Franc chuckled. "Guilty. Just thought I'd share a few developments… you know, compare notes."

For the next ten minutes, he outlined the event at the villa—the familiar faces, the unfamiliar ones, the mention of private inventory and insurance schemes, the forged sculpture, and lastly—the list.

Carly listened closely, only interrupting to ask for a name or a clearer description.

When he finished, there was a long pause.

"No official leads, then?" she asked.

"Not yet," Franc admitted. "But there are too many coincidences to stay quiet and I thought local records would help."

"Would this be the part where I say I'll scour through record offices, pull every favor I can, then meet you at the cafe?"

Franc smiled softly. "Not just yet. But I wouldn't discourage you from keeping the weekend open."

"Noted." Carly replied, assuming Franc believed she was in Bordeaux. Not that she needed to explain her downtime. After all, she would be open for the weekend as he'd wished.

They exchanged a few lighter words before hanging up, the kind that come from shared admiration and unspoken possibilities.

Carly called in her favors in Bordeaux to get the ball rolling.

After finishing his coffee, Franc threw on a light linen jacket, black Gucci sunglasses, and stepped into the sun-soaked streets of Nice. There was no destination—just a silent hope that the city might reveal something more to a man who knew how to watch.

He wandered the Cours Saleya market first—vibrant and fragrant with fresh flowers, olives, and fruit tarts. Locals bartered; tourists snapped photos. Franc purchased a small bag of candied citrus peel and a slice of pissaladière from a weathered vendor who claimed to have sold it to a French president once upon a time.

He took his time strolling through Old Town again, this had become an exercise routine challenging the hills with his stride. Always appreciating the painted shutters, the wrought iron balconies, the scent of fresh bread wafting through tight alleys. He noted several antique dealers and watch repair shops—one in particular with a window display that boasted two vintage pieces resembling those he'd seen in photos tied to stolen collections.

He jotted the shop's name in a small notebook. Just in case.

By midday, he found himself sitting beneath a yellow striped umbrella near the harbor, sipping chilled water and reading over his notes. The sunlight danced off the boats below, and while the view looked like leisure, Franc's thoughts were anything but idle.

Somewhere in the layers of elegance and sea salt, a truth lay hidden.

And Franc Merlot wasn't going to let it stay buried.

Chapter 13

Chips and Clues

Franc made the call just after noon, standing in the shadow of a statue in Place Masséna. The voice on the other end answered after a single ring—gruff, direct, unmistakably familiar.

"Franc Merlot. I wondered when you'd finally need my help again."

"Jean-Paul," Franc said, smirking. "Still betting on the long odds?"

"Only when I know the game is rigged in my favor."

The two exchanged a few lines of quick wit before settling on a meeting place: Café de Paris, Monte Carlo, tomorrow at one. Franc knew it well—an elegant terrace with perfect views of the casino and better views of the players. It was where information passed as smoothly as the chilled rosé.

Jean-Paul Duquesne had once been a professional croupier, but he had since elevated himself to something far more valuable—a human ledger of the region's undercurrents. He didn't just know who had money, but where it came from, how it moved, and why it was sometimes best hidden. If anyone could illuminate the underbelly of the syndicate Franc suspected, Jean-Paul could.

After hanging up, Franc returned to his hotel and began preparing.

The next day, the twenty-minute train to Monaco was comfortable and swift. The Riviera blurred by in coastal flashes—terracotta rooftops, turquoise water, hillside villas. Bounding off the train and up the staircases Franc emerged in the warm receptive air of Monaco.

By the time Franc stepped onto the polished walkways of Monte Carlo, it felt like another world. Glossier. Cleaner. Dangerous in its own perfectly tailored way.

He arrived at Café de Paris just before one o'clock. The maître d' nodded at the mention of Jean-Paul's name and led him to a prime table near the edge of the terrace, where the breeze carried whispers of money and mischief.

Jean-Paul was already there, comfortably sipping an espresso with the posture of a man who knew he had nothing to prove. His silver hair was combed back, his suit was linen and effortless, and his mirrored sunglasses reflected the ever-turning roulette wheel of Monte Carlo life.

"Still watching the world one bet at a time?" Franc asked, taking the seat across from him.

Jean-Paul grinned. "I love this place. The table always turns, my friend. But the house—" he tapped his temple—"always remembers."

They ordered lunch—steak tartare for Jean-Paul, salade niçoise and a glass of Bandol rosé for Franc. Conversation drifted through pleasantries before Franc leaned in.

"I need to know who's been playing under the table lately. Specifically, anyone connected to stolen timepieces, high-stakes art deals, and an American who went missing after spending time in Saint-Julien."

Jean-Paul's smile didn't fade, but his eyes sharpened.

"Now that," he said slowly, "is a story only a fool or a very brave man would chase down here."

Franc held his gaze. "And yet, here I am."

Jean-Paul tapped his fork lightly against the rim of his glass. "You're not wrong to come to me, but this game—this one's been running a long time. Hidden auctions. Backroom deals in yachts off Cap Ferrat. Art sold twice, paid for once. And as for timepieces? They're just a currency now. Quiet, traceable, but never obvious."

He paused, chewing thoughtfully before continuing.

"There's one name that keeps resurfacing. Not officially. Never on record. But whispered, like a superstition: L'Orfèvre. No one knows his real name. But if something rare disappears… he likely placed the first bet."

Franc jotted the name down. "Does Mario Blanc know him?"

Jean-Paul snorted. "Mario knows everyone. But whether he understands who he's dealing with— that's another matter."

They sat in silence for a few moments, each digesting more than food. Franc offered Jean-Paul a cigar as he clipped the end off a small Millenium cigar by Davidoff for himself.

"I'll pass, but good taste in Cigars my friend." Jean-Paul replied.

Finally, Jean-Paul added, "If you're chasing L'Orfèvre, you're going to need more than charm and intuition, Franc. You'll need luck. And maybe, someone who isn't afraid to lose something."

Franc toasted the edges of his cigar before lighting it and then sipped his rosé and let the thought linger.

He had already lost once. He didn't intend to again.

Chapter 14

A Suite with a View

With the name L'Orfèvre now etched in his mind like a fingerprint on a stolen watch, Franc knew his time in Monaco wouldn't end after lunch. He checked into the Hôtel de Paris Monte-Carlo just after three o'clock—a seamless luxury nestled beside the casino where fortunes and secrets changed hands as quickly as poker chips. The lobby's grand marble pillars and gleaming chandeliers framed his arrival like a scene from a bygone era.

He booked a corner suite, casually requesting a view of the Casino Square. The concierge nodded, recognizing a man who preferred both comfort and proximity. Once in the room, Franc took inventory. The suitcase he packed in Nice wasn't quite suited for a night under the principality's shimmering lights. No matter. He left the hotel shortly after, slipping into one of the adjacent boutiques to collect the necessary upgrades: a crisp navy blazer, tailored linen trousers, a silk pocket square with just enough flair, and a pair of black leather loafers meant for smooth floors and careful steps.

At the pharmacy, he grabbed the expected overpriced necessities—shaving cream, aftershave, a comb—and a cologne he didn't wear often, but knew left a note of understated confidence. The kind that lingered without needing to shout.

Returning to his suite, he took his time preparing. Monaco was a stage, and tonight, Franc intended to blend into the background while watching every act unfold.

Franc stood at the edge of the rooftop garden at his hotel in Monaco, the sea laid out before him in deep blue folds. A light breeze toyed with the collar of his linen jacket, and the fading golden light poured over the domes and facades of Monte Carlo. From this height, he could see the yachts bobbing below, nearly indistinguishable from one another in their polished perfection.

A couple beside him murmured in Italian about real estate—something about a bidding war and an off-market offer. Franc sipped his drink and pretended not to listen but tucked the details away. Monaco had its own economy of whispers, and tonight, the wind carried more than sea air.

By early evening, he was seated at the casino bar, sipping a well-poured Sazerac. The room buzzed with hushed tension—roulette wheels spinning, cards flipping, glances shifting like the tide. Fashion ran rampant in Monaco, but the casino added another level up as men paraded much younger women (arm candy) scantily dressed throughout the gaming tables. Franc noted every face, every dealer's smirk, every too-eager laugh from tourists trying to look comfortable in tuxedos. He didn't come to gamble. Not tonight. He came to listen.

Later, he'd move outside to the local high traffic evening stops—Jimmy'z, then maybe Buddha-Bar. He'd wander through the night like smoke—slow, quiet, lingering where others overlooked. Names were starting to swirl. And if L'Orfèvre truly operated in the shadows of this golden playground, Franc would be one step closer to bringing him into the light.

A productive evening warranted a deep sleep. Franc woke after the sun but quickly ordered room service for his usual coffee vice.

Outstanding service arrived only moments later as he chased down the double espresso and croissant then readied himself to take to the streets again. He expected the daylight hours and crowds to differ drastically from the high society he'd encountered last night.

After a quick glance at the newspaper while ordering another double shot from the lobby barista, he set out on foot.

The changing of the guard ceremony at the Palace Square in front of the Prince's Palace scheduled promptly at 11:55am would be Francs first destination.

Next, Franc wandered through a tucked-away gallery in the old quarter of Monaco-Ville. He hadn't intended to stop, but the curved ironwork sign caught his eye—Galerie du Sud. Inside, an older man with sharp features and silver cufflinks nodded in greeting.

"You're not here for the Van Houtens, are you?" the man asked, voice smooth as oiled leather.

"Not today," Franc replied. "Curiosity, mostly."

"Curiosity in Monaco is either expensive or dangerous." The man smiled. "Or both."

Franc glanced toward a framed photograph of a vineyard—too familiar. He drew closer. A small brass plaque read: Estate Collection, Gironde Region.

Interesting, Franc thought. Very interesting.

Franc found a small cafe servicing the local fresh catch and paired it with the waiter's recommendation of a white grape Rhine region Riesling from Germany. Franc complied, without regret.

On his walk back toward the casino, Franc passed a man seated at a quiet café terrace—tweed jacket, leather gloves, a single red rose pinned to the lapel. He seemed both misplaced and completely at home.

The man raised his espresso in a silent toast as Franc passed.

Franc slowed slightly. He had the feeling he'd seen the man before, perhaps at the art gala, or the yacht party, or even in a photograph… somewhere.

He didn't stop, but he made a mental note: Rose lapel. Café D'Azur.

In Monaco, subtle markers were rarely just fashion.

Chapter 15

Silence in the Vines

Franc traversed the hills of Monaco with his usual unhurried stride, letting the afternoon sun guide him through the winding streets that curled above the glittering coast. There was something satisfying in the way the city clung to the cliffs— old stone staircases that seemed to rise out of nowhere, ivy-covered walls, and sudden glimpses of yachts far below like toys on a satin-blue ribbon.

He knew his purpose but allowed himself those little moments of indulgence—a café noisette on a breezy terrace, a stop inside a gallery where the owner was too eager to share details of a recent private sale to a man with no known background but an appetite for obscure Italian pieces. After all, every lead somewhere and he needed answers. Franc noted everything.

It was always the same pattern: art, wine, rare timepieces. High-end luxury items moving through untraceable hands. When something can't be tracked, it usually shouldn't be.

By early evening, he found himself checked out of his posh hotel and near the station. The quick train back to Nice was due soon, and he'd gathered enough whispers to keep his thoughts busy for the rest of the ride. As the city of princes faded behind him, he leaned back and considered what awaited him next—not in Nice, but north.

Carly's search was picking up pace, as she had returned to Bordeaux looking for a few unanswered questions.

She had taken over a small corner of her favorite wine bar, papers and an old laptop spread in front of her as a curious waiter topped off her glass of Merlot. Her digging into Le Domaine de L'Argentière had turned up more than she expected.

The vineyard had been passed down through generations—quietly, without fanfare—until five years ago when a Luxembourg-based holding group, under the name Saphir et Cendre, acquired it. The locals weren't pleased. A few smaller vineyards had claimed that border markers had been adjusted in the years since, with vines they believed to be theirs now under the new owners' control.

One vintner she spoke with—old, proud, and sharp—said plainly, "They didn't buy the land. They bought the silence."

And then, tucked deep in a regional archive, she found a copy of a civil filing. A neighboring property had filed a legal protest at the time of sale, arguing that Le Domaine de L'Argentière had improperly claimed mineral rights along the southern ridge. The protest went nowhere. Quietly dropped. Settled out of court—or off the record entirely.

Carly sat back, staring at the screen.

The vineyard wasn't just a place for tastings and sunsets. It was ground zero for something deeper—an intersection of old money, ancient grudges, and modern ambition. Beneath the surface of its picturesque charm and rows of golden vines lay layers of tension and territorial resentment that had been simmering for decades.

Her recent findings had peeled back the romantic veneer. The land the vineyard sat on had been under quiet dispute for years, tangled in a mess of inheritance claims, suppressed sale records, and a recent acquisition by a holding company with murky ties. What seemed like a simple transaction had, in truth, left a trail of bitterness. And now, that bitterness has become dangerous.

The former owners hadn't just lost a vineyard. They'd lost legacy, leverage, and in some cases, livelihood. Some had gone quietly, others less so.

There were rumors of intimidation—land agreements signed under pressure, and some witnesses who'd abruptly left town. Carly's research even unearthed whispers of forged deeds and questionable court rulings that tipped the balance in favor of the new company.

She picked up her phone and dialed Franc. He answered on the second ring, just stepping off the train in Nice.

"I've got something," she said without hesitation.

"So do I," Franc replied, already walking toward the promenade. "Looks like L'Orfèvre has long fingers and a taste for old things—art, watches, wine… land."

She nodded to herself. "We may be circling the same fire, Franc."

She shared her thoughts as Franc circled town listening, fascinated at her discovery.

For Franc, this changed everything. What had appeared as an unrelated patchwork of clues— the missing American, the elite art circles, the high society yacht parties—were now part of the same tapestry. The vineyard was at the center. A symbolic crown jewel, yes, but also a practical one—an asset too valuable to lose and too contested to hold peacefully.

He realized then: the vines didn't just run deep in the soil—they ran deep into the veins of everyone connected to them. And Carly's findings had placed them both in the path of people willing to do anything to protect what they considered theirs.

He paused, watching the sea darken under the evening sky.

"Then let's see who gets burned."

"Maybe a train ride is in order again." Franc joked to her.

She agreed.

Chapter 16

Charts and Currents

Carly returned to Nice just before noon, the following morning, her scarf caught in the breeze as she stepped onto the platform with a purpose in her stride and a leather-bound folder pressed tightly beneath her arm. Franc was already waiting, leaning casually against a pillar, espresso in hand and sunglasses shielding his gaze.

"You travel light," he said, offering the slightest smile as she approached.

"I travel fast," she replied, tapping the folder. "And I brought the weight where it counts."

They settled into a shaded café not far from the port, the Mediterranean stretching beyond them like a painted stage. Carly laid the folder open on the table between them, flattening out maps, land transfer documents, and a series of marked photos.

"The vineyard's acquisition wasn't just a financial transaction," she began. "It was a strategic play. Borders were blurred, local families forced to surrender land they swore was theirs, and all with backing from companies that don't officially exist."

Franc took a long sip of coffee. "Sounds like someone was laying groundwork for something far more lucrative than wine."

She nodded. "And get this—the vineyard held a private tasting last year. Invite-only. Guests included two known art dealers, a Swiss banker currently under investigation for offshore laundering, and—" she flipped to a guest list copy— "a name with initials only: L.O."

Franc raised an eyebrow. "L'Orfèvre?"

"I'd bet a bottle of 1982 Margaux on it."

He leaned back in his chair, watching the sunlight dance across the harbor. "It's all converging—art, land, and now, a yacht party. No better place to move money or goods unnoticed."

Carly sipped her drink, her voice low. "And it's this weekend. Same luxury yacht we heard mentioned when the American went missing. The invitation was quietly extended to a list of 'investors'—which conveniently includes a Monaco wine broker we know."

Franc nodded slowly. "Then we go. Together."

"I figured you'd say that." Carly smirked, already pulling out her phone. "I've got us in. A friend of mine manages catering and slipped our names onto the guest manifest. I'm listed as an importer's representative. You—"

"Let me guess," Franc interrupted. "Security consultant?"

"More like… vintage procurement specialist."

He laughed, the sound light but fleeting. "Let's hope we don't become part of the vintage collection."

They agreed to meet later that evening to go over final details and plan their approach. Carly, always thinking ahead, had already made arrangements for attire fitting the upscale affair. Franc, not one for tuxedos but fully aware of the need for presentation, resigned himself to letting her choose.

As they stood, ready to part ways for a few hours, Franc glanced back at the open sea. Something about it tugged at his gut—a whisper of old memories and unspoken questions.

"You ready for this?" he asked.

Carly adjusted her sunglasses. "Only if you are."

And with that, they stepped into the current together, where truth bobbed just below the surface—and danger waited at every swell.

Early the next morning Franc decided it was time for a little reconnaissance before attending the yacht party. He called Carly with an address to meet.

Tucked into a shaded corner of a waterfront café, Franc and Carly sat beneath a fluttering white awning as the Mediterranean breeze stirred the linen napkins and carried the scent of sea salt and grilled seafood. Their espresso cups clinked lightly against porcelain saucers as they leaned in just slightly, the way people do when the conversation isn't meant for passing ears.

"That woman at the marina," Carly said, stirring a touch of sugar into her coffee, "she was rehearsed. Didn't flinch once when you probed about ownership."

"She's done it a thousand times," Franc replied, his eyes scanning the harbor beyond. "And yet, she stumbled—only slightly—when she mentioned the owners of that sleek Italian yacht at the end of pier four. Did you catch it?"

"I did," Carly said with a smile. "And that name she used—I've seen it before. Possibly in the vineyard acquisition documents."

Franc nodded, his eyes squinting in a concentrated and focused look for a moment as he swirled the last sip of his espresso.

Carly relaxed back in her chair, letting the sun warm her shoulders. "It all seems so well-manicured out there. Money buys charm, privacy, and protection. But something about tonight's gathering… I don't think it's just about champagne and sailcloth."

"It never is," Franc said, reaching for the small notebook he'd tucked into his coat pocket. He jotted a single word: Observe. "We'll keep our distance. Smile. Toast. Blend in. But we're there for a reason."

Carly tilted her head. "And if we're wrong?"

"Then we'll enjoy the wine and move on. But I don't think we're wrong."

She grinned. "I never think we're wrong either. I'm just playing devil's advocate."

The waiter returned with a dish of olives and small bites of toasted bread brushed with olive oil and tomato—just enough to tide them over until the evening's indulgences.

As they nibbled and watched the yachts shift in their berths, the mood between them was steady—calm before the storm. The calm of knowing too much already, and still not enough

From the second-tier balcony of a neighboring hotel, behind the shade of a half-closed louvered window, a pair of eyes lingered on the waterfront café. A camera lens, modest but expensive, rested on a cushioned tripod just behind the glass. The shutter clicked once—quiet, quick, unnoticed.

Franc and Carly, seated comfortably and sipping their espresso, looked no different than any other well-dressed couple enjoying the Riviera air. But the observer knew better. Their visit to the marina hadn't gone unmarked. The quiet questions, the way Franc had angled himself to get a better look at a certain crew member—these weren't the behaviors of idle tourists.

The man behind the lens leaned back, lips tightening into a thin line. He reached for his phone, tapped out a message in silence, then deleted it before hitting send. Timing, after all, was everything.

Below, Carly tilted her head at something Franc had said, laughing lightly, unaware of the frame they had just filled in someone else's story.

And just down the promenade, leaning on the polished railing near the gelato stand, another figure in sunglasses and a loosely tailored jacket appeared to be watching the yachts. But every so often, he adjusted his stance, just enough to keep the café within his peripheral vision.

For the past hour, an unease pricked at his neck. Franc had felt a strange weight in the air earlier as they had approached the cafe, something he couldn't place. Like a feeling of being watched but he couldn't confirm the notion. They sat alert hoping for a break. Knowing now enough of what to expect upon arrival at the evening's party. And just how to blend in.

Being under surveillance, especially where wealthy individuals participated in social activities was just par for the course Franc played.

Chapter 17

The Gathering Tide

The late afternoon sun cast long golden fingers across the Nice marina as Franc stood before the mirror in his hotel room, adjusting the lapels of his lightweight linen blazer. Crisp white shirt, no tie—just enough formality to blend in without drawing attention. Carly had insisted on coordinating their looks for the party. She'd chosen an elegant yet understated navy dress with pearl accents, paired with a silk wrap she could easily discard if the sea breeze picked up.

He slipped his watch on—an older Patek Philippe, discreet yet refined. The kind of piece that would earn a nodar from the right kind of company, but not enough flash to raise suspicion. Carly knocked lightly at the door, then entered without waiting.

"You look… intentionally forgettable," she teased, giving him a once-over.

Franc smirked. "Exactly what the occasion calls for. And you?"

She twirled slowly. "Blendable. But I've already spotted the weak links in the herd—too much perfume, jewelry clinking like silverware. The real power players never announce themselves."

Their earlier escapade shed light on the pre party festivities which offered them subtle concealment upon arrival.

They made their way down the cobbled streets toward the dock, following a stream of finely dressed men and women, laughter and champagne glasses already filling the air before they reached the water's edge.

The yacht, L'Ombre Blanche, was a floating palace—sleek, modern, and utterly without markings. Franc noted the lack of a visible flag, a telltale sign. Everything about it suggested discretion and money.

A red carpet lined the ramp leading up to the main deck, flanked by two well-dressed but serious security guards with earpieces. Guests flowed freely on and off the boat, some clearly mingling more than once before disappearing into the upper levels or returning ashore to adjacent lounge setups—pop-up tents, cigar bars, and velvet rope enclosures spilling onto the dock.

Carly handed over their names to the hostess, a woman with flawless posture and an expression that gave away nothing. With a practiced nod, she waved them forward.

They stepped aboard, the gentle sway beneath their feet reminding them they were no longer on land. Music played softly from somewhere—jazz, smooth and intentional. Waiters moved like choreographed dancers, offering glasses of chilled rosé, while clusters of guests exchanged quiet pleasantries in French, English, and the occasional Italian or German.

Franc and Carly fit the dress code impeccably and drifted naturally into the flow of guests, their ears open, and eyes sharp.

He leaned toward Carly, murmuring behind his glass, "Start by the bar. Look for the wine broker from Monaco. He's our best shot at a solid lead."

Carly gave the slightest nod and peeled away, her posture effortless, with a warm smile. She was practiced at this, her charm often disarming enough to loosen even the most sealed lips.

Franc made his rounds along the lower deck, stopping occasionally to comment on the vintage selections or strike up brief, seemingly innocent conversations. He spotted several familiar faces from prior dossiers—an art dealer known for moving questionable pieces, a hedge fund executive recently scrutinized for hidden offshore accounts, and, finally, a man Franc only knew from a blurry surveillance still—L'Orfèvre.

Tall, white-haired but youthful in posture, L'Orfèvre wore a tan jacket over a cobalt blue shirt, no tie, and thin sunglasses that barely hid his ever-moving eyes. He wasn't talking much, just nodding, always watching. He seemed to know exactly who everyone was and where they stood in the game.

Franc kept his distance, noting who approached L'Orfèvre and how long they stayed. Transactions of some kind were being made— but they were invisible to the untrained eye. A whispered word, a folded napkin exchanged, a signal in the direction of a steward.

Carly returned just before sunset, a low whisper against the din of conversation.

"The Monaco broker was here. He left about twenty minutes ago, but not before confirming something interesting—this yacht's owned by a silent holding group. Guess where they're registered?"

Franc raised a brow.

"Bordeaux. And guess which vineyard is their only listed asset?"

He didn't have to answer.

Carly continued, "One of the stewards confirmed a private tasting will take place in an hour below deck. Invite-only. High-value guests only."

Franc's eyes narrowed. "Time to earn that invitation."

They didn't come to drink, or dance, or drift. They came to observe.

And tonight, the tide was turning.

Chapter 18

If the Cellar Walls
Could Talk

As the sun began to dip below the horizon, casting the yacht in an orange-gold glow, the mood aboard L'Ombre Blanche shifted. The guests grew more animated, their conversations lighter, more flirtatious as the evening wore on. But for Franc, the party was merely a backdrop, the subtle hum of luxury and wealth just noise masking his sharper instincts. Carly, always in tune with the ebb and flow of such events, was already scouting the room for signs of those who might hold the keys to the puzzle—Anyone looking for an angle in the crowd.

The steward who had mentioned the private tasting earlier appeared again, this time with a knowing smile and a discreet invitation for Franc. It was simple, almost too casual: "Mr. Merlot, the tasting is beginning. If you'd like to join."

With Carly at his side, they followed the steward down to a lower level, past opulent rooms with walls lined in dark wood, antique furniture, and sparkling chandeliers. The air grew cooler as they descended into the private wine cellar, its walls lined with shelves of rare bottles and old vintages that could fetch millions at auction.

Inside the cellar, a long table was set, laden with glasses, decanters, and half-opened bottles of wine. A few high-profile guests were already present, gathered in small clusters, conversing in hushed tones. At the far end of the room stood L'Orfèvre, now without his sunglasses, his sharp eyes scanning the room like a hawk. His presence here wasn't just about wine, it was about influence, about power.

Franc and Carly moved to the bar at the back of the room, where the bartender was busy preparing a round of cocktails. Carly leaned in close, her voice low. "I spoke with the Monaco broker again. He confirmed what we suspected—L'Orfèvre's vineyard in Bordeaux is part of a larger operation that's involved in more than just winemaking. Money laundering, syndicate connections… It's all there."

Franc nodded, his mind racing. The vineyard, the holding company, the connections to Monaco—it was all coming together in a way that felt almost too convenient. This was more than just a search for a missing person; this was about an underground network of power, wealth, and influence that stretched from Bordeaux to the south of France, with threads leading back to some very dangerous people.

"Do you know who else is here tonight?" Carly asked, her eyes scanning the room.

"Not yet," Franc replied, his gaze fixed on L'Orfèvre. "But I plan to find out."

As if on cue, the man himself turned toward them, his lips curling into a polite, practiced smile. He walked toward them with an air of both command and elegance, his movements deliberate, calculated.

"Mr. Merlot," L'Orfèvre greeted, extending a hand. "It's a pleasure to finally meet you. I've heard much about your… work."

Franc shook his hand firmly, but his mind remained sharp. "The pleasure is mine, I'm sure. This is my colleague, Ms. Provost."

Carly offered a polite smile, her hand lingering just a moment too long in his.

L'Orfèvre's gaze flicked between them, taking in the subtle tension. "I must admit, I didn't expect to see such distinguished guests aboard tonight. Perhaps you're here for more than just wine, Mr. Merlot?"

Franc allowed himself a slight smile, keeping his tone neutral. "I find that wine, like people, can often reveal more than one expects."

L'Orfèvre chuckled softly, his eyes flicking to the glasses in their hands. "True enough. But let's see what tonight's selection offers."

They joined the group around the long table, where several other notable figures had begun to gather. The sommelier, an older man with a refined air, began to pour the first wine—a rare vintage from a vineyard in the Médoc region. The discussion turned to the subtlety of terroir, the uniqueness of the harvest, and the craftsmanship behind each bottle. Franc listened intently, but his attention was divided, flicking from one person to the next.

The guests' conversations remained light, but beneath the surface, there was a sense of calculation. Everyone here had a purpose. Some were simply there for the pleasure of the wine, others had their own agendas. Franc's mind raced as he noted the figures in the room—there was the Monaco broker, the art dealer he had spotted earlier, a few powerful figures from the business world, and, of course, L'Orfèvre.

But it wasn't until the third wine was poured, a deep red from the heart of Bordeaux, that Franc noticed something that caught his attention.

A man, standing near the back of the room, lingered in the shadows. He was older, his clothes understated yet expensive, his eyes hard and calculating. Franc couldn't place him at first, but there was something familiar about the way he moved, the way he observed. Then it hit him— this man wasn't just a guest. He was someone who operated behind the scenes, pulling strings without ever making his presence known.

He leaned closer to Carly. "Keep an eye on that man," he murmured. "Something about him doesn't sit right."

Carly's gaze followed his. "I see him. I'll make my way over."

Franc stayed back; his mind sharp. The pieces were beginning to fall into place, but they were still scattered. He needed more—more information, more connections. And soon, he'd find out who the real players were behind this syndicate.

The tasting continued, but Franc's focus had shifted. He wasn't just a guest anymore. He was a man on a mission, surrounded by people who were playing a game far more dangerous than he'd anticipated.

And tonight, he would get one step closer to uncovering the truth.

She moved with intention gracefully, understated, and almost too composed for the setting. Franc noticed her before she even reached him, her silken navy dress catching the light just enough to make her presence known without demanding it. A wide-brimmed hat dipped slightly over one eye, but not so much as to obscure the sharp intelligence that flickered behind her gaze.

"Mr. Merlot," she said softly, just above the hum of conversation around the tasting table. Her accent was unmistakably French, but her tone suggested she'd spent time in many places, refined and layered.

Franc turned slightly, his demeanor calm but alert. "Yes?"

She didn't smile. "I won't stay long. I've already been noticed." She placed a folded slip of heavy cream-colored paper on the edge of his plate. "If you're still interested in the American and what he might've seen, this should help."

Franc's eyes flicked down to the note, then back up to her. "And what's your stake in all this?"

She hesitated just a beat. "Let's just say I've seen too many good people disappear. And too many bad ones remain comfortable."

Before he could ask more, she turned and disappeared into the low light of the cabin— swallowed by silk, perfume, and whispered conversations. Franc watched her vanish, then slipped the paper into the inside pocket of his blazer without drawing attention.

Carly returned to his side moments later, brows raised. "Who was that?"

Franc's look drawn ever so slightly. "Someone who doesn't want to be noticed… but very much wants to be heard."

He signaled the steward for another glass of wine. Whatever the note contained, he would wait to read it. Timing was everything. And tonight, the game was shifting.

The headline dominated the front page of the morning gazette:

"Local Authorities Detain Suspect in Riviera Art Theft—Stolen Piece Recovered During Surprise Raid."

Franc stood outside the café with a hot espresso in hand, scanning the article. Carly joined him moments later, brushing sleep from her eyes, her own copy of the paper folded beneath her arm.

"They moved fast," she said, noting the date on the stolen piece—just three weeks ago. "But what are the chances the arrest happens the same night we're aboard a yacht with half the region's elite— and during an art showing?"

Franc nodded. "Either an incredible coincidence or someone's nerves snapped with the extra attention last night."

He looked back down at the grainy image printed in the center of the story: a man partially obscured by a coat being ushered into an unmarked vehicle. No name was released yet, only that he was found in possession of "an item believed to match the missing piece from a private estate near Èze."

"What do you think?" Carly asked, eyes narrowing. "Inside job?"

"Or someone got too bold," Franc muttered. "And perhaps… he wasn't supposed to be at the party."

Carly sipped her coffee. "You think he was there?"

Franc didn't answer right away. His fingers tapped the newspaper lightly, lost in thought. Then he looked up, eyes sharp again.

"If he was, someone in that crowd saw him. And someone wanted him out of the picture before anyone else started asking questions."

They both turned toward the marina, where the morning light danced off the moored yachts.

"Let's see who's still in town," Franc said. "And who's suddenly gone quiet."

Chapter 19

The Walls Are Closing In

Mario Blanc stood in his small but tastefully cluttered apartment above a wine boutique just off Rue Masséna. The smell of last night's cologne and the faint aroma of espresso clung to the air. The morning sun sliced through the linen curtains, landing squarely on the crumpled copy of the Nice Matin Gazette spread out across his kitchen table.

He rubbed his temple, blinking the residual fog of wine and gossip from his mind. The headline stared back at him. Art Theft. Yacht Party. Arrest.

He hadn't spoken to Franc at the gathering—too many prying eyes, too much risk—but he had seen him. Had seen Carly, too. And more importantly, he'd seen someone else. Someone who didn't belong in that kind of crowd. He couldn't quite place the face. Not yet. But it had bothered him all night.

He tossed the paper aside, the unease in his chest nudging at something unspoken.

Mario showered quickly and selected his usual blend of unbothered charm and studied elegance—tan linen blazer, no tie, subtle gold timepiece, and freshly polished loafers. He checked his hair in the mirror, gave a slight smirk, and stepped out into the Nice morning, the streets already humming with café chatter and scooter engines.

Down the block, he bought a second paper and tucked it under his arm as he turned toward his usual café—Le Cendrier Bleu—where the owner didn't ask questions and the espresso was strong enough to stir old memories. He needed to think. He needed to remember who that man was at the yacht party—and why the look in his eyes reminded him of a story he once overheard in a back room in Monaco… something about a vineyard, a forged canvas, and a man who disappeared before the ink could dry.

He couldn't tell if the threads were pulling together or unraveling completely. But he knew one thing.

Whatever had been set in motion, it had reached him now.

Mario stirred his espresso slowly, watching the thin ribbon of crema dissolve into the dark liquid like a secret slipping beneath the surface. The café was quiet—locals speaking in hushed tones about the arrest, their voices dancing between curiosity and caution. He sat alone, leaning back in the wicker chair, letting the breeze carry in the salty tang from the sea.

He wasn't just reflecting. He was remembering.

That man—the one at the yacht party—had been standing near the upper deck's champagne bar, speaking softly with a small cluster of guests. But it wasn't his voice or posture that caught Mario's eye. It was the ring.

A heavy gold band with a green stone—unmistakable to anyone who'd been in Monaco's art scene long enough. It had belonged to an old gallery patron, a recluse named Fabien Langlais, who'd vanished five years ago after a failed auction scandal and whispers of stolen work. But the man wearing the ring last night? Much younger. Smoother. More careful. He was no ghost of Langlais, but Mario wondered if perhaps he was the shadow left behind.

He reached for the folded newspaper and scanned the article again. No name. No confirmation. But the piece recovered had been traced back to a private estate—and that same estate, Mario now recalled, had once been connected to a holding company. The same name Carly had mentioned when Franc called her about the vineyard.

He scribbled something on his napkin:

Langlais – estate – holding co – Bordeaux.

Underlined twice.

Finishing his espresso, Mario stood. He paid in cash—always in cash—and left the café with a half-smile at the barista, who returned it with a wink.

Rather than heading to his shop or back to the apartment, he walked aimlessly toward the old harbor. If what he suspected was true, then the vineyard, the art theft, and the man on the yacht weren't just tangled in coincidence. Someone was laundering stolen pieces through property and wine—using heritage and exclusivity as the perfect mask.

And Franc? He was circling closer than anyone had in years. Too close.

Mario took out his phone and hesitated. Then he sent Franc a single message:

"I think I've seen the ring before. Fabien Langlais. Call me."

Then he turned toward the port, the sun sharp on the water and the air beginning to pulse with the heat of the day.

Things were moving now. Faster than expected.

Chapter 20

A Message from the Margins

Franc and Carly sat beneath a striped awning at La Petite Table, a quiet bistro tucked off the promenade. It was just past one, and the lunch crowd was thinning—locals retreating to shaded courtyards, tourists migrating to their next coastal distraction. A bottle of chilled rosé sweated between them, half-drunk, as they picked at Niçoise salads and shared conversation that had finally, for a moment, turned personal.

"So," Carly asked, tilting her sunglasses down just enough to look Franc in the eye, "are we ever going to talk about that woman who approached you on the yacht, or are we pretending it didn't happen?"

Franc smirked, wiping the corner of his mouth with his napkin. "Nothing to tell yet. But I have a feeling we'll see her again."

Carly rolled her eyes, but the smile lingered.

That's when Franc's phone buzzed. He casually reached for it, expecting a reminder, maybe a news alert. But instead, one word blinked at him like a whisper from a darker room.

Mario.

He opened the message.

"I think I've seen the ring before. Fabien Langlais. Call me."

Franc's posture shifted. He set the phone down without speaking and stared past Carly toward the open street, as if suddenly aware of how visible they were.

Carly noticed immediately. "What is it?"

He hesitated, then showed her the message.

She read it silently, her lips pressing into a thin line. "Langlais? I haven't heard that name in years." Her eyes narrowed. "Why now? Why Mario?"

Franc leaned back in his chair; the sunlight painting patterns through the awning across his jacket. "That's the part I don't like. He was at the yacht party. Didn't say a word. Now suddenly he wants to help?"

Carly looked over her shoulder instinctively, lowering her voice. "Or lure you in."

"I've considered that," Franc said, swirling his wine. "But there's something in the name Langlais that rattles me. He vanished after the auction scandal. There were rumors he escaped with more than just money—pieces never catalogued. The kind that disappears into the world of private trades and backroom galleries."

"And now," Carly added, "one shows up… and the man with a connection to the vineyard is wearing his ring?"

Franc nodded slowly. "Exactly. Which makes Mario's sudden tip-off—what? A warning? A peace offering? Or a trap?"

Their server appeared with the bill, sensing the shift in tone. Franc paid quickly, his thoughts already racing ahead.

"We'll call him," Franc finally said as they stood. "But not today. Let's let him sweat a little. If this is a setup, I want him to wonder how much we know too."

Carly nodded, falling into step beside him. "And in the meantime?"

Franc slipped on his sunglasses. "We find out everything we can about Fabien Langlais… and who might be wearing his ring."

They left the café, the light around them bright and breezy, but the space between their thoughts thickened with every step.

Chapter 21

The Root of the Vines

The midday sun cast a golden haze over the streets of Nice as Franc made his way down a narrow back alley near the archives building, his coat slung over his shoulder and a thin folder tucked beneath his arm. Inside were copies of land deeds, transfers, and articles tied to the vineyard he had once wandered without suspicion—back when it was nothing more than a peaceful retreat with Carly and a few passing tourists.

Now, it looked increasingly like the ground had been bought with more than grapes in mind.

The name that kept repeating in the documentation: Vespera Holdings, a seemingly innocuous company with little online footprint. On paper, they held parcels of land in Provence, Bordeaux, and a few scattered regions near the coast. But the more Franc dug, the more names he began to recognize—shell companies connected to the art world, offshore trusts, and most recently, a financial exchange involving a vineyard just outside Saint-Julien… the very one he and Carly had toured together.

Franc stopped by a quiet café to spread the documents across a small table. He took a slow sip of coffee, scanning names and numbers. There it was again—Langlais. Not Fabien this time, but a woman—Colette Langlais, listed as a one-time partner in the holding group prior to its restructuring.

He jotted the name into his notebook and circled it twice.

Just then, his phone buzzed again—this time from a private number. He answered cautiously.

"Merlot," he said plainly.

A woman's voice responded, low and elegant. "If you're looking for Vespera, you're already late. But if you're looking for who planted the seed at that vineyard, then we should talk."

Franc's eyes narrowed. "Who is this?"

A soft laugh. "Someone who wants to see what grows when the right soil is turned. You'll find me at the bookshop on Rue Colbert in one hour."

The line went dead.

Franc sat back in his chair, the echo of the voice lingering like perfume. A new piece on the board. Another thread pulling tight.

He closed the folder, dropped some euro on the table, and stood.

If the vineyard was a cover, it had grown more than grapes—it had grown secrets. And now, someone was finally ready to harvest them.

Franc made his way to Rue Colbert, the pace of his steps, intentionally somewhere between a stroll and a mission. The streets here had a different feel—quieter, more insulated, with little storefronts leaning into the road like they had secrets of their own. The scent of aged paper and brewed herbs seeped from one of the awnings ahead, and Franc instinctively knew he had found the right place.

The bookshop bore no formal sign, only a modest gold lettering on the glass that read "Livres & Légendes." The aged wooden oak and glass door creaked open at his touch, and the cool scent of worn book bindings and wood polish welcomed him in.

She stood next to a floor lamp near the back wall, casting her long shadow into the aisle of lined books, as she casually thumbed through a weathered hardcover novel. Tall, poised, wearing a wide-brimmed ivory hat and dark red gloves that seemed more for elegance than warmth. Franc recognized her from somewhere—perhaps a gala in Marseille years ago, or a whispered name in an old case file. This was Colette Langlais.

"You came," she said without looking up. "Good. I dislike speaking to men who ignore invitations."

Franc stepped forward, careful with his words. "You've got my attention."

She finally looked up, her eyes a piercing gray-green. "The vineyard is part of a much larger dispute, Inspector—or should I say, former Inspector. When we sold it, the intention wasn't cultivation, but consolidation. Land ownership is an influential tool here. And influence… well, you've found out where it can lead."

Franc's jaw tensed. "Art theft? Disappearances? A syndicate hiding behind terroir and barrels?"

Colette smiled faintly, as if amused by his phrasing. "All true. But not all of it begins in Nice, nor ends in Saint-Julien. You're circling a truth too dangerous to name, which means you're close."

He leaned in slightly. "Who's L'Orfèvre?"

At this, Colette's expression dimmed. "The Forger. But not just of art—of identity, of provenance, of legitimacy itself. He doesn't steal; he rewrites history. And yes, his reach has touched the vineyard. You walked the land. You saw the hidden cellar, didn't you?"

Franc froze. "I didn't think much of it at the time."

"You should have." Colette handed him a small envelope. "Inside is a name. It's not his, but it's next door. Knock carefully. L'Orfèvre surrounds himself with mirrors and shadows. One wrong reflection, and he'll vanish."

Franc nodded slowly, tucking the envelope inside his jacket. "Why help me?"

Colette turned back to her book. "Because I've seen what happens when no one stands in his way. Consider this… my atonement."

Franc left the shop without another word, his mind racing. As he stepped out onto the street, the world seemed brighter, too bright—like the curtain had lifted, and beneath the wine and charm of southern France, something ancient and calculating stirred.

He called Carly.

"Pack your bag," he said. "We're heading back to Bordeaux."

Chapter 22

The Return to the Vines

Carly met Franc at the train station just after noon, a neutral-colored trench tied loosely over her shoulders, a crossbody satchel bouncing lightly with each step. She had questions written across her face, but trusted Franc enough to let him lead—at least until they reached Bordeaux.

The train ride was quiet, a blur of coastlines, vineyards, and exchanged glances. Franc was unusually still, hands clasped in front of him, the envelope from Colette still unopened. He waited until the rhythm of the train smoothed into a hum before pulling it from his coat and carefully sliding out a folded card.

The name written in bold script simply read: "Dumas Fillion." Beneath it, a note: Caretaker. Historian. Loyal to a fault.

"Dumas Fillion?" Carly echoed after Franc read it aloud. "That name's tied to the estate, isn't it?"

Franc nodded. "I saw it once on the corner of an old map—next to the cellar entrance. He's either been guarding secrets… or enabling them."

By the time the train arrived in Bordeaux, the skies were threatening rain. Gray clouds hung like sagging curtains above the station. Franc flagged a taxi, and within the hour, they were pulling up the long gravel path that curved gently around the familiar hills of Château Des Vents.

Despite the overcast sky, the vineyard was golden—rows of vines stretching neatly toward the horizon, heavy with mid-season fruit. The estate house was still, save for one figure tending the side garden near the main gate.

Franc stepped out first. The figure stood and wiped his hands on a towel before walking toward them.

"You're looking for Dumas?" he asked without hesitation.

Franc offered a polite but firm nod. "Franc Merlot. This is Carly Provost. We have a few questions."

Dumas tilted his head thoughtfully. His face was lined with age, but his posture still bore the discipline of someone used to responsibility.

"I assumed someone would come eventually," he said. "The cellar, I take it?"

"And the previous ownership," Franc added. "Particularly the holding company involved in the last transfer."

Dumas didn't flinch. Instead, he motioned toward the rear of the estate.

"There's something you need to see. Follow me."

Carly looked at Franc as they trailed behind the caretaker. "Why do I get the feeling this is going to make things even more complicated?"

Franc's voice was low. "Because when secrets hide underground, they usually grow roots."

They followed Dumas to a moss-covered stone path that led behind the estate. He stopped at a door nearly invisible behind hanging ivy. With an iron key that looked older than Franc's first case, Dumas opened the door to a cool, earthen corridor.

"This isn't a wine cellar," Dumas said. "It was once a meeting place for the estate's former owners. Then, it became something else. When the holding company took over, they left me instructions—preserve the space, deny access to outsiders."

"Why?" Carly asked, her voice echoing slightly in the low ceiling.

Dumas flicked a switch. Weak yellow bulbs came to life along the walls, revealing a long hallway lined with old ledgers, crates labeled in several languages, vintage wine bottles with mismatched vintages… and an ornate framed canvas covered in cloth.

Franc stepped toward the painting. He didn't touch it.

"That's what they stored here?" he asked.

Dumas nodded. "One of many. But that one was meant for someone specific. A man they called L'Orfèvre."

Carly moved closer. "So, he was here. In Bordeaux."

"More than once," Dumas said. "And if I may…"—he looked at Franc—"there's something else. This estate wasn't just a storage facility. It was a transfer point. A place to legitimize false provenance. Swap labels. Create stories for things with none."

Franc took a breath. "And the American who disappeared…?"

Dumas hesitated. "He was here. Asking too many questions. But I haven't seen him since."

Outside, the sky finally broke, rain tapping lightly on the old slate roof above. Franc glanced at Carly, then back at the painting.

"I think it's time we lifted the cloth."

With a slow hand, Franc pulled the cover away.

And what stared back wasn't just a painting. It was a forgery. A nearly perfect one—of a missing Monet.

Carly whispered, "So this is what they've been hiding."

Franc stared at it in silence.

"No," he said. "This is just the beginning."

Chapter 23

Beneath the Vines

Franc sat on the edge of a weathered stone bench near the estate's rear garden, the rain now just a mist weaving through the late afternoon light. The chaos of the last few weeks—the stolen art, whispers of forgery, unexpected party invitations, discreet warnings from mysterious women, and Mario's clumsy presence—had swirled like an unsolvable riddle.

But now, for the first time, it all made sense.

He lit a cigarette, letting the silence and the moment carry him through the final connections. Not everything was a lie—just enough of it to steer a curious mind in the wrong direction. And he, of all people, should have seen it coming sooner.

They'd fed him just enough of the art trail to distract him. Watch collectors, high society drama, forged paintings buried beneath estates. A dramatic orchestra of culture and deceit. But it had all been noise.

The truth was simpler—older, more rooted. The American hadn't disappeared because of art or crime. He'd vanished because he was asking the wrong people the right questions… about land.

About this land.

The vineyard wasn't just wine and nostalgia. It was a legacy. It was a position. It was power. And the holding company that acquired it, quietly and without reverence for its local legacy, had upset a delicate balance that had existed in the hills of Bordeaux for generations.

Someone had wanted that American to be quiet. Maybe not permanently—but at least long enough for deals to close and records to vanish. Franc had seen that look before in boardrooms and underworld meetings alike: power cloaked in civility.

And Mario? His involvement, if any, had been peripheral. Guilty of proximity and poor judgment, but not malice. A man who moved in circles where secrets were currency and appearances were everything. He'd panicked, maybe helped hide something… but he wasn't the architect.

Franc stubbed the cigarette into the wet stone.

Carly approached from the far side of the garden, holding two coffees. She passed him one without a word, sensing he was close to the end.

"I've been thinking," he said finally. "Every time we got close to the truth, something loud happened. A party. A painting. A paper headline. But they overplayed their hand."

Carly took a slow sip, her eyes locked on his. "So, what's next?"

Franc stood, the weight of everything lifting just slightly from his shoulders.

"Next?" he said. "We try to find the American."

He looked toward the vineyard house—the heart of this century-old deception.

"Because if he's still alive, he knows exactly why he was silenced. And if he's not… someone here made sure we'd never find out."

A breeze swept through the vines, shifting them like a whispered warning.

Franc straightened his coat. "Time to rattle the roots."

Chapter 24

The Roots Revealed

Franc and Carly returned to the vineyard just after midday. The summer sun bore down with the kind of heat that made the stone walls radiate the past. Franc wasn't interested in the wine today. He wanted documents, names, deeds—the dry pieces of paper that told more truth than any wine cellar tour or estate history ever could.

Inside the modest estate office, an elderly clerk named Antoine remembered Franc from his recent visit. Franc kept the tone polite, even warm, as Carly sifted through records alongside him. The holding company's name—Domaine Nouvelle Héritage—stood out like a fresh scar across decades of lineage.

Carly pointed to one particular acquisition form buried under years of minor transfer papers. "Here," she said. "The American's name. He was a broker, not a tourist. He wasn't passing time— he was mediating a private counteroffer for another buyer."

Franc's eyes furrowed a wrinkle on his forehead. "And someone didn't like that."

Antoine, eager to remain neutral, gave a careful nod. "This land has always had strong opinions surrounding it. Outsiders… aren't always welcome, even if they come with money."

It confirmed everything Franc suspected. The American—now confirmed to be working under a pseudonym—had been closer to closing a sale on a large piece of the estate that certain families didn't want sold. His disappearance wasn't just about real estate. It was about preserving generational status.

They exited the estate without fanfare, both knowing now that they weren't chasing shadows anymore.

Back at the hotel, Franc's phone lit up with a message from Mario:

"Any updates? Please call me. I have a bad feeling."

Franc stared at the screen for a long moment. He knew Mario had been squirming ever since the art theft arrest at the yacht party. That world—the one Mario moved through with practiced charm—was beginning to crack. He likely feared being implicated, even as a bystander.

Franc slipped the phone back into his pocket without responding.

Let him squirm.

Mario had chosen his games. He'd sidled too close to secrets for comfort, and Franc had no interest in giving him the relief of absolution—not yet.

That night, Franc and Carly dined on the hotel terrace. The sea was calm, and the stars arrived without a rush. They spoke little, the kind of silence shared between people who had uncovered more than they wanted, yet felt they were just beginning.

"There's still the matter of the missing man," Carly said, finally breaking the quiet.

Franc nodded. "But now we know where to look—and who's invested in us never finding him."

The waiter refilled their glasses, and Franc raised his toward her. "To digging deeper."

Carly clinked hers softly against his. "To finishing what we started."

Chapter 25

A Man, Misplaced

Franc stood near the café window, sunlight scattering through the tall panes, casting long lines across his table. He reread the message again, even though he already had it memorized.

Subject: Confirmed. The American is alive.

Location: St. Petersburg, Florida.

Alias used: "James Denham"

Actual name: Gregory Caldwell

He blinked once, then looked over the rim of his espresso toward Carly, who sat opposite him scrolling her phone, equally stunned.

Carly set her phone down, half laughing. "So… Gregory Caldwell just walked away?"

"Seems that way," Franc said, setting his cup down with a soft clink. "After realizing the vineyard was a powder keg and that he was the fuse, he faked a convenient disappearance and skipped town."

Carly shook her head, grinning. "And somehow everyone here decided it was a conspiracy, a kidnapping, a cover-up—or all three."

"In fairness," Franc replied, leaning back, "some of it was a conspiracy. Just not the part involving his vanishing."

They both chuckled, a much-needed release after weeks of shadows, stolen paintings, fake names, yacht parties, and whispered threats. The truth, as always, had been hidden in plain sight—but ironically, it had also already taken a plane back to Florida.

Gregory Caldwell was now back in his glass-walled office in downtown St. Petersburg, comfortably operating under his real name. A neat little law practice. An assistant who answered calls. A framed diploma. Not quite the life of a man who'd once tangled with French land disputes and vineyards worth generations of grudges.

Franc shook his head in amusement. "He vanished himself. It wasn't abduction—it was avoidance."

Carly raised her glass of wine. "To Gregory Caldwell, the only man to disappear, scare half of Bordeaux, and end up at a smoothie shop next to a dog groomer in St. Pete like nothing ever happened."

Franc clinked her glass. "To resurrecting the living."

As the sun dipped lower over the French Riviera, the air turned golden and soft. The kind of moment that made you forget how many loose ends still floated just beyond the horizon. Franc didn't mind. There would always be more. But for now, a good laugh, a glass of wine, and the knowledge that the mystery had been solved—even if its missing man had just been cleverly… ordinary—was enough.

Franc stood at the balcony of his Nice hotel suite, the Mediterranean breeze brushing lightly against his collar as he sipped a perfectly chilled glass of Sancerre. Below, the city moved at its usual elegant pace—tourists lingering outside cafés, scooters weaving between cars, and the occasional sound of laughter rising like steam into the sky. But Franc wasn't laughing. Not yet.

His phone buzzed again on the marble-topped table behind him. Another message from Mario. That made three—each vague, cryptic, but unmistakably laced with panic.

Franc narrowed his eyes.

There was a time when he would've called Mario back immediately, eager to chase down any lead. But now? He had learned something in all his years of peeling back layers: sometimes silence reveals more than conversation.

Mario had been around the periphery of this mess for too long. Always present, always listening, always claiming innocence while walking just close enough to danger to raise suspicion. Franc didn't doubt Mario's involvement anymore—at least, not in some capacity. He wasn't sure whether the old restaurateur was orchestrating something, covering for someone, or simply tangled in the web of wealthy secrets and backdoor deals that often bloomed under Riviera sunshine. But he was sure of this: Mario was sweating.

And Franc liked that.

Let him wonder. Let him sit in his silk robe and fidget with his espresso, wondering if the net was drawing tighter. Let the silence stretch.

Franc turned back to the sea, the rim of his wineglass catching the late light. For now, he would play it his way. The land dispute, the holding company, the fake names and the missing American—it was all starting to settle into place. The picture was finally coming into focus.

He picked up his phone, glanced at Mario's message, then locked the screen and slipped it into his pocket. Not today, Mario. Let the suspense do the talking.

Franc smiled. This was a part of the job he didn't often admit enjoying. The moment when the hunter stopped chasing—because the prey had already started to tremble.

Mario, of course, would read the news two days later and pour himself a double.

And Franc? He never called him back.

Chapter 26

The Last Pour

The soft hum of conversation filled the shaded terrace of Le Papillon d'Or, one of Nice's most timeless cafés nestled on a quiet street where old vines wrapped around wrought iron railings and the scent of rosemary clung to the warm afternoon air. Franc Merlot swirled a glass of deep red, the color of sunset on stone walls, and watched the way the light played on the surface. There was something poetic in that—how even the most stirred waters settle again.

Across from him, Carly sat with her sunglasses pushed atop her head, a small smirk on her lips. "I've already booked my train back to Bordeaux," she said, resting her chin in her palm. "Unless you have another yacht party to crash or another fake disappearance to solve."

Franc smiled without looking up. "No more yachts. No more missing Americans. No more vineyard intrigue—at least not this week."

They sat in comfortable silence, watching the world pass, familiar faces of the Riviera brushing past them like ghosts from previous chapters. The art dealers, the heiresses, the watchmakers with secrets. Mario had yet to call again, and Franc had still not returned the message. That silence, he decided, said more than any confrontation ever would.

He pulled out a folded sheet of paper from his inside pocket and laid it on the table. A copy of the property transfer record for the disputed vineyard. Highlighted were the names of silent investors. Shell companies. Trails designed to mislead.

"I'll file a quiet note with a friend of mine in Paris," Franc said. "Nothing formal. But enough to stir the right minds. Let the bureaucrats untangle what's left."

Carly reached for the paper but paused. "You're letting it go?"

He nodded. "The truth's out. Or enough of it, anyway. The rest? It's wine-stained politics, old grudges and greedy hands in velvet gloves. But the man's alive, and the vineyard… will find its own peace or burn in its own ambition."

Carly leaned back, satisfied. "So, what's next?"

Franc took a sip, savoring the vintage. "Maybe I go home for a while. Trim the vines. Mend a fence. Maybe I don't chase the next case. Maybe a holiday is in order. I've never been to Florida." He smiled. "I hear Disney World is exciting."

She laughed. "You always say that. And don't even think about vacation or going to Florida."

He raised a brow. "And yet here we are."

The afternoon lingered, lazy and golden. Franc glanced across the square to where an elderly couple shared a cone of gelato, the woman wiping a smudge from the man's cheek. A group of tourists passed, snapping photos of a mural Franc had stopped noticing years ago.

"I think I finally understand something," he said softly.

Carly leaned in. "What's that?"

He looked at her, eyes sharp but content. "Some mysteries aren't meant to be solved. Some are meant to be understood."

And with that, he raised his glass one final time.

"To the missing," he said.

Carly clinked her glass gently against his.

"And the found."

Epilogue

The wind rolled softly over the hills of Bordeaux, carrying with it the scent of turned soil and early grapes. Franc Merlot stood at the edge of the vineyard, the very one that had quietly unraveled so many truths beneath its sun-soaked rows. He looked out over the land—not just as a detective, but as a man changed by what he had uncovered.

The American, alive and back to his world in Florida, had left behind more than confusion. His supposed disappearance had been the perfect distraction, one orchestrated by those who feared exposure over a long-buried land dispute. The art thefts, the whispers in Nice, the tangled affairs in

Monaco—all threads meant to mislead and protect the deeper truth.

Carly walked up beside him, a glass of wine in hand, her expression half amusement, half admiration. "We followed paintings and parties," she said, "but we found a vineyard war."

Franc smirked. "Seems appropriate. Nothing in this region is just wine and leisure."

They both knew the story wasn't entirely over. Some names had remained hidden, others only half-exposed. But for now, the dust had settled, and the land stood quiet—still contested in spirit perhaps, but no longer a weapon masked behind forged contracts and false disappearances.

Mario Blanc, for his part, had kept a low profile since Franc had chosen not to return his final message. A silent punishment that likely stung more than any confrontation.

The vineyard breeze shifted again, and Franc took a slow breath. It wasn't the end of all mysteries, but it was the end of this one. And that was enough for now.

He turned to Carly. "Lunch in town?"

She nodded, smiling. "Only if you let me choose the wine."

"Deal," Franc said. "But I reserve the right to correct you."

As they walked away from the rows of vines, the sun dipped lower, casting long golden shadows. The Vintage Vendetta had come to its close—not with dramatic fanfare, but with quiet truth, good wine, and the certainty that some things—like the land and the past—are never quite done speaking.